Arthur, For the Very First Time

Arthur, For the Very First Time

Patricia MacLachlan

Illustrations by Lloyd Bloom

SCHOLASTIC INC.
New York Toronto London Auckland Sydney

"The Mockingbird" by Randall Jarrell. Reprinted with permission of Macmillan Publishing Co., Inc. from *The Lost World* by Randall Jarrell. Copyright © Macmillan Publishing Co., Inc. 1963, 1964. Originally appeared in *The New Yorker.*

ISBN 0-590-46530-9
ISBN 0-590-29113-0 (meets NASTA specifications)

Text copyright © 1980 by Patricia MacLachlan. Illustrations copyright © 1980 by Lloyd Bloom. All rights reserved. Published by Scholastic Inc., 730 Broadway, New York, NY 10003, by arrangement with HarperCollins Children's Books, a division of HarperCollins Publishers.

1 2 3 4 5 6 7 8 9 10   40   00 99 98 97 96 95 94 93

Printed in the U.S.A.

First Scholastic printing, April 1993

For all my family—
but especially for my mother, Madonna

Contents

Arthur, For the Very First Time

Moles

The summer that Arthur Rasby was ten years old was a problem summer. During the daytime his mother and father argued. At night they whispered loudly. Also, the downstairs toilet hummed and wouldn't stop. The plumber, a woman in overalls the color of vanilla pudding, came to fix the hum. She banged, poked and stuck her head down the tank. The hum went on, though.

"Do you like your job?" asked Arthur politely. He perched on the edge of the bathtub taking notes in his journal.

"Until now," said the plumber grumpily.

After the plumber left, Arthur kicked the toilet hard and the humming stopped.

Then moles came to visit the Rasby lawn. At least that's what Arthur's father said they were. He showed the crisscross of humped lines on the lawn to Arthur.

"What do moles look like?" asked Arthur.

"Ugly," said his father.

Arthur wrote in his journal:

Moles: ugly

"And they always come no matter what I do!" said his father angrily.

Ugly, but loyal,

wrote Arthur. *A nice quality,* he thought.

When Arthur asked more questions, his father yelled and threw a shovel against the garage. It left a brown mark on the white paint, which made his father even angrier.

Arthur sat a long time beneath the honeysuckle bush waiting to see a mole. He wondered if moles had humming toilets and grumpy fathers too. Did they have small unseen creatures burrowing in *their* lawns? He put his ear close to the ground hoping to hear the sound of scrambling feet, or at least flushing, but all he saw was a black ant carrying a large white crumb. He smoothed a grass path for it so it wouldn't stumble.

Arthur's father came out of the house and put his hand on Arthur's head. "Let's fix ourselves something for dinner," he said. "Mom's not feeling well."

Arthur knew that this was his father's way of saying he was sorry for yelling about moles.

"What is there to eat?"

"Chipped beef," said Arthur's father, and they both laughed.

They went inside, holding hands.

"Are you lonely this summer?" asked Arthur's father as they ate peanut-butter-and-lettuce sandwiches.

Arthur's friends had all gone to camp or to visit their grandparents. But Arthur knew what his father really meant. He knew his mother was going to have a baby. He just didn't want anybody to know that he knew. Nobody had told him. But he thought he knew the signs. His mother stopped to babble and ogle at babies—strange babies. It was embarrassing. She spent her mornings in the bathroom being sick, which, Arthur thought, was the trouble with the toilet. She got far-away looks on her face. "What?" she asked Arthur idly when he asked her a question. "What did you say?"

Arthur knew that his father would want him to like the idea of having a brother or sister. But Arthur didn't. Babies were not human. They made monkey sounds. You couldn't talk to them. They grabbed things and wet their pants and threw up all over everything. Arthur knew. He had made a study of babies. He had an entire narrow-lined notebook full of observations on babies. And he didn't want one.

"No," Arthur said to his father. "I'm not lonely. But I sure would like a pet rat. A white one with a long pink tail."

"A white what?" asked Arthur's mother, standing at the kitchen door.

"A white rat," Arthur told her with some satisfaction. He knew how his mother felt about rats. He watched her bathrobe billow out behind her as she fled to the bathroom.

And so it was that Arthur came to stay with his Great-Aunt Elda and Great-Uncle Wrisby the summer of his tenth year.

"They'd like to have you," said his mother.

"There's lots to do there," said his father.

And Arthur went to his aunt and uncle's house while his parents went off to practice not yelling at each other.

On the way to his aunt and uncle's, Arthur took out his journal to see what he had written about them. When he had been seven, he had written one entry under their name.

> **Their house is big like a manshun. It smells like banas.**

He corrected the spelling to read "bananas" and stared a bit at "manshun." Arthur had been almost a baby when he'd written that. The thought made him squirm. He wondered if he'd been a monkey-babbling, wet, grabbing baby.

"Here we are," called his father. Arthur heard a strange note of excitement in his voice.

The house was immense. Arthur smiled. Some things

didn't change from when he was seven years old. Once he had revisited a mountain, only to find that when he was ten years old the mountain was only a small hill. The house reached back over the land like someone stretching, its wings on either side like arms thrown back. Arthur wondered if it would still smell like bananas. Arthur could see Uncle Wrisby's famous garden in the side yard, planted in alternate rows of onions and roses. No one had ever known why he planted such a garden. Maybe no one had ever asked. Arthur made a note in his journal to find out why.

Uncle Wrisby loped out to the car, tilted slightly forward as if he had a wind at his back. He was uncommonly tall, with a small head much like a graying tennis ball. It perched on top of his body precariously, as delicate as the gold-rimmed glasses that rested on his nose.

He bent down to peer in the car windows. "Come in, come in," he shouted. He was hard of hearing, so he yelled. Everyone who talked to him yelled, too, even though Uncle Wrisby read lips very well.

"Coming!" called Arthur's father. "We're coming!" Arthur's mother put her hand to her head. Arthur made a note to research whether the yelling would reach the baby inside her.

They climbed out of the car as Aunt Elda came hurrying out from the left wing of the house. She was shaped like an uncertain circle, made up of large shifting spaces like an easy-to-color coloring book. Her yellow-white hair was coiled over her head in fat braids that fell as she ran. She stopped several times to pick up the combs that had fallen along with her braids. She was followed closely by a russet-colored chicken. Each time Aunt Elda stopped, the chicken stopped, pecking at the ground. When Aunt Elda ran again, the chicken ran, too.

"That's Pauline," said Arthur's father with a mysterious smile.

"Pauline?" asked his mother.

Aunt Elda reached the car, her braids down her back and Pauline not far behind. "Arthur!" she said, holding his shoulders. "You're not a baby anymore." That, at least, was to her credit. Arthur liked her immediately.

Pauline pecked cruelly at his mother's shoelaces, forcing her back into the car. "I don't think we can stay," she called from inside. She was afraid of Pauline.

Pauline, frustrated, went over to peck at Arthur's father's shoes. He bent down.

"Hello, Pauline. How are you—*comment vas-tu?*"

Pauline stopped suddenly and tilted her head to gaze up at him. She came over to peck about Arthur's feet.

"Say something in French," said his father softly.

"*Bonjour,* chicken," he said. Pauline pondered Arthur, cocking her head to one side.

Arthur's mother sighed from the car.

"I think we'll go along," said his father. "Arthur's things are all here."

Arthur went over to his mother's side. "I'll be here," he said.

"I know," she said, reaching out of the car and hugging him close. "I love you, too."

"Au revoir," he said to his father over his mother's shoulder. His father looked very pleased as he drove off.

"Come, come," yelled Uncle Wrisby. "We'll have something to eat. Then we'll talk about the world and its workings." He took hold of Arthur's hand. "What would you like to talk about?"

Arthur stared at Uncle Wrisby. Here was someone who wanted to talk about things! With him!

Arthur opened his journal. "Moles!" he cried happily. "Let's talk about moles!"

His pencil poised, the summer began.

The Far Away End

The house was a book, and Uncle Wrisby and Aunt Elda the characters. From the moment that Arthur walked in the front door, he was a new character . . . a willing captive in the life story of his aunt and uncle. He noted, recorded and stored in his head the old colored-glass windows, the long hallways and the worn stairways with sunshine at the top.

Aunt Elda sat Arthur at a round oak table in her kitchen. Its legs were chicken feet that grasped round balls.

"Here's your list, Arthur. Check off the food you don't like, and we'll see what we can do about it."

"You mean I won't have to eat what I don't like?" Arthur asked. He thought about tuna-noodle casserole and spinach that grew cold on his plate.

"I said we'll see what we can do about it," said Aunt Elda.

The list was in alphabetical order. Arthur had

checked asparagus and cauliflower when Uncle Wrisby appeared from behind an old door next to Aunt Elda's black iron stove.

"Explore, Arthur," he shouted. "You can pick the bedroom you want."

"I can?"

"Go on!"

Arthur checked off eggplant, green peppers, spinach, then quickly, zucchini, and went to explore. He passed from room to room, opening doors, finding new rooms beyond. The house seemed endless. And it was full of things to look at and go back to later: shelves of books, rock specimens, deep chairs warm as cocoons and pictures of laughing people whom Arthur had never seen before. He liked their faces. There were many staircases and small alcoves lined with windows of wavery glass turned lavender from years of sunlight. And on the very top floor, Arthur found his room. He knew it when he opened the door. The room was large, with a window seat and tall windows. At one end was a small brick fireplace. In it were brass andirons with tops cast as sailing ships. At the other end of the room was the high bed, with a small stool by one side. Arthur climbed up. A quilt made up of many-colored squares covered the bed. On each square was a sailing ship; some were single-masted sloops, some ketches, some schooners. From where he sat, Arthur could see out the windows. The branch of a large tree almost touched the windowpane, and through the leaves he saw a river as it snaked down from the hills through the valley. Far in the distance were meadows with cows and sheep feeding.

"So you found your room," called Uncle Wrisby from the doorway. He walked to the closet door and opened it. There stood Arthur's suitcase and knapsack.

"How did you know?" cried Arthur.

"I knew," said Uncle Wrisby matter-of-factly.

Pauline walked around the door, then flew over to settle in a rocking chair.

Uncle Wrisby and Arthur laughed.

"*Bonjour,* Pauline. *Tu es très intelligente.* It looks like Pauline knew, too," said Arthur's uncle. He sat on the window seat and leaned toward the windows. He pointed a long finger at the nearest roof.

"That's the Hotwater house," he said. "And there's the MacAvins' and behind that is Reverend Railbaugh's garden . . ."

Arthur ran to the closet to get his journal.

"What's that you're doing?" called Uncle Wrisby.

"My journal," said Arthur.

"Journal?"

"Like a diary," explained Arthur. "I write about people, things I see, everything I think about."

"Everything?" Uncle Wrisby looked at the notebook suspiciously. "You got me in there?"

"Maybe," said Arthur, smiling. "Didn't you ever write in a journal, Uncle Wrisby?"

"Nope," said Uncle Wrisby, shaking his head.

"Never. Don't believe anything written. Only what I see." He sat for a moment looking out the window. Then, abruptly, he stood up and went to the closet.

Arthur studied the wallpaper. There were scenes of a sea village, with church spires and hills going down to the water.

"I've got these instead of a journal," said Uncle Wrisby. He took a pair of binoculars out of a leather case. "I can see way down the valley road and know what's going on. When people are up close enough, I can even tell what they're saying sometimes."

"You can?!" Arthur slid off the bed.

Uncle Wrisby opened the windows and leaned way out into the leaves of the tree. Arthur grabbed his uncle's belt.

"There, there you can even see that scatty man, Yoyo Pratt," yelled Uncle Wrisby.

Arthur tugged at Uncle Wrisby's belt. "Who? Why is he scatty?"

Uncle Wrisby came back through the window. "Not your business."

Not his business! No one had ever said that to Arthur before. Everything was his business. He knew all kinds of secrets. He knew about Piggy Rathbone's father's secret false teeth. He knew about his Uncle Charles pinching women. He knew about his mother having a baby.

Uncle Wrisby handed the binoculars to Arthur.

"Look in the little end if you want to see things close

up," he said. "The other end makes everything far
away."

"Far away? Why would you want to see things far
away?" asked Arthur.

"Sometimes you see just as well," said his uncle. He
looked at Arthur thoughtfully. "Sometimes better."

"Dinner!" called Aunt Elda from the bottom of the
stairs.

"Come on, Arthur," said Uncle Wrisby. "Let's go eat
Aunt Elda's weed crisp."

"I heard that," said Aunt Elda from below. "Just
because I put herbs in the pot."

Arthur and his uncle went down the many stairs and
through the hallways to the warm kitchen. The room
smelled of applewood fire and rose geraniums. Pauline
perched on a stool near Arthur and watched him eat,
tilting her head in brisk movements. For dessert they
ate dark-chocolate pudding with warm cream. And
when he was full, Arthur laid his head on his arms and
listened sleepily as Aunt Elda and Uncle Wrisby talked.

There was darkness at the windows when Arthur felt
himself being carried up to the high bed. He felt Aunt
Elda's hair brush his cheek when she tucked him into
bed, and he knew Pauline was walking on the bedspread.

"Pauline, *viens,*" whispered Aunt Elda. Arthur felt
Pauline hop from the bed, and he heard the small
scratching sound of her feet against the wood floor.

When it was quiet, Arthur made his eyes open. He

saw the moon through the tree. *Why would anyone want
to look through the far away end?* he asked himself. Then he
slept, dreaming of brass sailing ships, ice-white waves
topped with spindrift and green-wallpaper hills that
sloped to the sea.

The Mockingbird

There was feathered warmth by Arthur's head. He
awoke to see Pauline sitting on his pillow. She pushed
her long neck down and pulled at a tuft of his hair.

"Stop. *Arrêtes*, Pauline," said Arthur, laughing. She
settled down on the quilt, satisfied that he was awake.
He put out a hand and stroked her smooth back. He
was fascinated by the staccato movements of her head.

He reached for his journal.

> **Monday, June 7: Pauline—my friend. French—why?
> Uncle Wrisby says moles are not ugly. They are secre-
> tive.**

He jumped from the bed and sat in the window seat,
reaching for the binoculars. Pauline followed him, settling on the wide windowsill.

The gravel road that passed the house was bordered
by low stone walls covered with wild honeysuckle.

Arthur knew about honeysuckle. He knew that you could suck the sweet juice from inside when it was in bloom. His mother had taught him that. He put down the binoculars, frowning, thinking about his parents. And then, slowly, he turned the binoculars around to look through the far away end. He moved the glasses carefully, studying the distant pattern of meadow and woods, now so far away yet strangely clear. He saw a small pond off to one side of the river surrounded by brush, and he watched the movement of birds swooping out over the water, nervously, as if they knew they were being seen.

Suddenly, a dark movement in the tree outside interrupted his view. Arthur put down the binoculars. The movement was a bird with black at the eyes, like dark pencil marks.

Arthur heard a noise behind him, and turned to see Aunt Elda standing in the doorway.

"Aunt Elda." He beckoned her. "What's this bird?" He turned back quickly, and the sudden movement frightened the bird to a higher branch.

Aunt Elda sat by Arthur.

"There." He pointed.

Aunt Elda smiled. "Oh, that's my mockingbird. He sits high up at the very tallest part of the tree or on the chimney. He sings every other bird's song and his own. He imitates."

"He does?"

Aunt Elda nodded. "He goes on and on, especially at

mating time. He lets all the other mockingbirds know that this is his territory." Aunt Elda reached up to take the combs from her hair. "But the best thing of all is how he lures his mate to his nest. He places something in his nest that he thinks the female will like."

"Like what?" asked Arthur. "How do you know?"

"We're old friends," said Aunt Elda. "I know what he wants." She let her long hair down the length of her back, and from her pocket she took a small pair of scissors.

"This is what the bird likes," she said. And she cut a long hank of her hair. "Here," she handed it to Arthur. "Put this out at the crook of the tree and watch."

"But your hair!" said Arthur, awed. "There's a big space there."

"Never mind," said Aunt Elda with a wave of her hand. "I never miss it. I always look the same." She opened the window. "Go on," she said. "Climb out and watch."

Arthur's mouth felt dry. Dry with fear. He'd never climbed this high before. Never for himself. Never for a silly bird.

"No," he said, his voice sounding high and tight. "No," he repeated softly, looking helplessly at Aunt Elda.

She regarded him steadily, then smiled. "Then I will," she said. "You can watch this time."

This time, Arthur thought. *No. Never anytime.*

Aunt Elda climbed out on the windowsill and then

onto the sturdy limb. "Notice the bark, Arthur," she said over her shoulder. "It's sycamore. Notice the spots?"

This made Arthur smile. Smart old lady. She knew he was afraid. But she didn't seem to care.

"Nice bark, Aunt Elda," he called. "Nice bark."

Aunt Elda reached out, thrust the handful of hair in the crook of the tree so that it wouldn't fall. Then she slowly turned around, lifting her arm once to wave at Uncle Wrisby, who was working in the side garden.

"There now," she said as she climbed back in the window. She beamed at Arthur as though she had climbed to the edge of the earth. Well, hadn't she?

"You watch, now, and before the day is over he'll come for the hair." She patted Arthur's arm lightly. "Breakfast in a few minutes." She stopped. "Would you like to eat up here in the window?"

Arthur nodded, looking at the hair at the crook of the tree.

Aunt Elda went, humming to herself, down to the kitchen, and Arthur stopped watching the hair to write in his journal.

Aunt Elda did the strangest thing today. She climbed out on the big tree and put some of her hair there for a bird. She *says* he'll use it for his nest.

Arthur leaned out the window and peered down at the grass, then at Uncle Wrisby hoeing in the garden. He picked up his pencil.

> **I've never really looked at bark before.**
> **The grass below seems smooth, like an ocean. But if you look closer you can see each blade of grass and every leaf that has fallen.**

Aunt Elda came with a tray of eggs and toast. She brought cocoa for Arthur and tea for herself. Her hair was coiled up on her head again, and what she had said was true: She looked just the same.

"The bird has been coming for a long time," she told Arthur. "And every year I give him my hair. He brings his children to the big tree sometimes. I think they're his children. He teaches them the songs of the other birds." She waved her hand toward the barn. "We planted multiflora roses there; the berries feed him all winter. And there's black alder, too." She smiled. "It shows red berries against the snow in winter."

Aunt Elda put down her tea and opened a book.

"There's a wonderful poem about the mockingbird," she said. "Listen." And Arthur stopped eating as she read Randall Jarrell's poem.

> *Look one way and the sun is going down,*
> *Look the other and the moon is rising.*

The sparrow's shadow's longer than the lawn.
The bats squeak: "Night is here"; the birds cheep: "Day
*　is gone."*
On the willow's highest branch, monopolizing
Day and night, cheeping, squeaking, soaring,
The mockingbird is imitating life.

All day the mockingbird has owned the yard.
As light first woke the world, the sparrows trooped
Onto the seedy lawn: the mockingbird
Chased them off shrieking. Hour by hour, fighting hard
To make the world his own, he swooped
On thrushes, thrashers, jays, and chickadees—
At noon he drove away a big black cat.

Now, in the moonlight, he sits here and sings.
A thrush is singing, then a thrasher, then a jay—
Then, all at once, a cat begins meowing.
A mockingbird can sound like anything.
He imitates the world he drove away
So well that for a minute, in the moonlight,
Which one's the mockingbird? which one's the world?

There was a long silence in the room. Both Aunt Elda
and Arthur stood, watching the hair at the crook of the
tree. Finally, Arthur began to say something. But Aunt
Elda stopped his talk with a whisper.

"Hush. Look."

The mockingbird fluttered to the big branch. Pauline

made a small clucking sound, and Aunt Elda put a comforting hand on her back. The bird sidled his way down the branch toward the crook and looked at the hair. Arthur felt himself smiling. Then, before Arthur's next breath, the bird grasped the hair and flew. His white wing streaks shone brightly in the early light. He flew up over the barn, wheeling high with the length of hair rippling behind him like the tail of a kite. Then he disappeared.

"Same old mockingbird," said Aunt Elda softly. "Praise be."

Arthur explored the yard and barns that afternoon. He watched Uncle Wrisby in the garden and saw two rabbits feeding in the field. Uncle Wrisby showed him a huge rock near the back woods with a hole dug beneath.

"Our fox," said Uncle Wrisby proudly.

Pauline followed Arthur everywhere, flying up to perch on the fence as Arthur watched Uncle Wrisby's pigs rooting in the paddock. More than once, Arthur found himself watching the trees and looking up hoping to see the mockingbird. That night he wrote in his journal

> Aunt Elda climbs trees. High trees.
> Uncle Wrisby looks through the big end of the binoculars.
> I think *they're* scatty.

Arthur paused, looking through the window at the big tree.

I don't understand the poem, either.

But most of all, Arthur didn't understand the strong sense of excitement that he was feeling for the very first time in his life.

Come All Ye Fair

"Where does Pauline sleep, Uncle Wrisby? And why do you speak French to her?"

Arthur and his uncle were cutting up apples to make applesauce. But Uncle Wrisby was eating most of the slices.

"What if you eat a worm, Uncle Wrisby?"

"Amino acids, Arthur," said Uncle Wrisby, chewing.

"Is that a fancy name for worm juice?" asked Arthur.

"Now you tell me, does amino acids sound as bad as worm juice?"

"Pauline sleeps there. Behind the old stove," said Aunt Elda.

At one end of the old stove were stored the slabs of wood for feeding the fire. At the other end was a small cradle with a soft square of flannel. Pauline's name was carved at the head.

"*Viens,* Pauline! Bedtime. *Va dormir,*" called Uncle Wrisby.

There was a flutter at the top of the back stairs, and Arthur ran to see Pauline hop, step by step, down the stairs. She ran to her cradle, jumped in and pulled the small blanket over her with her beak.

Arthur hooted with delight. "Can I do it?"

"She'll do it for anyone," said Uncle Wrisby.

And it was true. No matter what time of day, no matter where she was, Pauline would come. Arthur would call, *"Viens,* Pauline. *Va dormir!"* and she would hop down the stairs, fly in from the yard or run from the front parlor, jump into her cradle and pull up her blanket.

"She likes to please," said Aunt Elda fondly. "She's a good chicken."

Thursday, June 10: Pauline is like a sister. Better than a sister! She's not babbly, not drooly. I love her.

"We speak French," explained Uncle Wrisby loudly, "because Pauline likes it best."

"The old coot likes French best," corrected Aunt Elda, sewing a button on Arthur's jacket.

"French is pretty," protested Uncle Wrisby. "Sweet to a chicken's ear!"

Aunt Elda snorted.

"Il pleure dans mon coeur comme il pleut dans la rue!" yelled Uncle Wrisby. "Do you know what that means? It weeps in my heart as it rains in the street. Isn't that sweet to the ear?"

"It'll rain in your pigpen if you don't get out there and throw some bedding down," said Aunt Elda.

"All right, all right," said Uncle Wrisby, shaking his head. "No romance in *that* soul," he said, pointing a long finger at Aunt Elda.

"And don't wear your galoshes in the house," she added. "They draw on your eyes."

Draw on your eyes, Aunt Elda says. Nobody ever told me that. My friend Jamie Baird wears rubbers everywhere. That's because he's a detective. RUBBER FEET ARE SILENT FEET his card says. Everybody says Jamie's eyes are deep set. Now I know why.

"Wait, Uncle Wrisby. Where are you going?"

"Out to see Bernadette," called Uncle Wrisby. "My pig."

"His girl friend," said Aunt Elda, ripping a piece of thread with her teeth.

"She'll be birthing in a while," said Uncle Wrisby. "She's lonely."

"Wait!" cried Arthur. "Wait for me."

"Nothing to wait for, boy," said Uncle Wrisby. "Only babies."

"Boy," said Arthur mostly to himself. "How right you are." And he ran off into the afternoon after Uncle Wrisby.

———————

Uncle Wrisby climbed over the fence into the pigpen and Arthur climbed after him. The paddock was muddy with small patches of hay here and there. Uncle Wrisby slogged through the mud, shooing off the smaller pigs, who ran, squealing and grunting. He stopped by a huge black-and-white pig who stood, head lowered, in a murky puddle of water. Uncle Wrisby bent down and murmured to her. And then he sat right in the mud, water licking his boots. Bernadette sighed, leaned and lay down, nestling her head in his lap.

Arthur picked his way, trying to step on stones and hay.

Uncle Wrisby scratched Bernadette between the ears, then he lifted his head and sang loudly:

> *"Come all ye fair and tender maidens,*
> *Take warnin' how you court young men."*

"Bernadette likes singing," he called to Arthur. "I've sung to her since she was a baby."

Uncle Wrisby sang that song about maidens to old fat Bernadette. I don't think Bernadette is any ye fair and tender maiden. And I know my mother wouldn't like me sitting in the mud.

"They're like a star on a summer's morning," Uncle Wrisby sang on. *"First they'll appear and then they're gone."*

Uncle Wrisby's voice was smooth and pleasant, and Arthur sat on a mound of hay, lulled by the song. Bernadette turned her head a bit and stared shrewdly at Arthur. She was just about the ugliest thing Arthur had ever seen, her wet, mottled snout jutting out from under sharp button eyes.

> *"I wish I was a little sparrow,*
> *And I had wings, and could fly so high."*

Arthur felt something by his elbow—a small flutter—and he turned to see Pauline. He lifted his arm and she sat, nestling warmly against his body. Arthur smiled and closed his eyes, the sun warming his face.

Here I am, he thought, *with my scatty uncle who sits in the mud and sings to pigs.*

Arthur's hand brushed along Pauline's body. And another thought intruded that caused him to open his eyes in surprise.

I wonder where the mockingbird's nest is, he thought. And for a moment, his binocular eyes turned inward on himself: a small boy, sitting on a hay mound with a russet chicken. Then he closed his eyes again and listened happily to an old man's song on a summer afternoon.

Starlings

The girl appeared like a starling on the fence: rumpled, unkempt and raucous. "Hey," she called to Uncle Wrisby. "What are you doing with that silly pig, Rasby?" Her legs dangled down, swinging back and forth. They were dotted with bruises and her socks had slumped in her shoes.

"Scratchin' and singin'," called Uncle Wrisby without looking up. "She likes it."

"And why does she like it?" prompted the voice.

"Because she's silly!" shouted Uncle Wrisby, and they both smiled at a familiar joke.

She jumped off the fence, and her shoes made sucking noises as she walked through the mud. The noise made Arthur wince. He thought about his mother. He thought about the new baby in a clean, white blanket.

She sat next to Uncle Wrisby and brushed her black hair out of her eyes.

"This is Arthur," said Uncle Wrisby loudly. "He's

come for the summer." He turned to Arthur. "This is Moira MacAvin. Her grandpa's the vet."

She looked at Arthur. Her eyes, he noticed, were as steady and shrewd as Bernadette's.

Uncle Wrisby began singing again. And Moira MacAvin stuck out her tongue at Arthur.

Arthur was shocked. Mazzy Lewis did this all the time. But he'd known Mazzy for three years. Moira kept it stuck out while Uncle Wrisby sang.

"I wish I was a little sparrow,"

(It stuck out.)

"And I had wings, and I could fly so high."

(It never wavered.)

Aunt Elda came out of the house and waved. The tongue disappeared.

"Moira," she called. "Moreover's coming by for you."

Bernadette was sound asleep now, snoring a bit. Moira and Uncle Wrisby got up carefully and walked to the fence, dripping mud and water. Arthur got up too, and began jumping from dry spot to dry spot.

"Don't forget, Rasby," said Moira. "One of the babies is mine."

"So you've said a million times," said Uncle Wrisby, grinning.

Aunt Elda smoothed Moira's hair.

"Here comes Moreover," she said, as a battered black car made its way up the hill. The car wavered back and forth across the road, brushing against bushes and bumping up on rocks.

"Old fool," murmured Aunt Elda. "He scars more trees driving."

The car came to a scraping stop, and Moreover jumped out to put a big rock in front of a back wheel. He looked just like Moira. *Another starling,* thought Arthur, *that had the same black, wild hair.* And Arthur wouldn't have been surprised to see him stick out his tongue.

"How's Bernadette?" he called to Uncle Wrisby.

"Gettin' ready slowly," said Uncle Wrisby.

"Better get her inside if it rains," said Moreover, "or she'll birth in water and you'll have the only floating litter in town. Moreover, you ought to line her stall with fresh hay. Moreover, you'll have to keep the other pigs away from her. Moreover, you must be Arthur," he said in the next breath.

"Come for the summer," said Uncle Wrisby, nodding.

"How do you do?" said Moreover.

"Fine, thank you," said Arthur.

"Fine, thank you," repeated Moreover, folding his arms. "Listen to that, Moira. Why can't you talk like that?"

"Because I'm not fine, thank you, most of the time,"

said Moira, tossing her hair. "Most people aren't, if you ask me. If most people told the truth they'd say, 'I'm feeling poorly, if you must know. My gout's bad, I've got earaches and leg pains and my stomach burns like poison; my teeth are dropping out by the sevens . . .'"

Moreover began chasing Moira about the yard. She raced for the paddock.

"'. . . and my skin's breaking out with the fungus,'" she called over her shoulder.

"You wild rascal!" shouted a grinning Moreover.

Moira leaped the fence.

"'And I've got dropping scabs and was bit by a rabid muskrat,'" she yelled as she tripped in the mud.

One of the young pigs came over to nose about just as Moreover managed to crawl over the fence and began tickling Moira.

"How *are* you, Moira?" he shouted.

"Fine!" she shrieked.

"Fine what?" he asked.

"Fine, thank you!"

Moreover looked up.

"Now did you all hear that?" He sat up. "She's fine, thank you. Moreover, I believe she means it!"

He stood up and pulled Moira up after him. He took a chain from his pocket and looked at his watch.

"Almost five o'clock. Got a call at the Hotwaters'. Come on, Moira."

They climbed back over the fence, and Aunt Elda

made clucking noises and dabbed at their mud with her apron.

"What's wrong at the Hotwaters'?" she asked.

"Their dog," announced Moreover. "He smells awful and burps."

"We must invite him for dinner," commented Uncle Wrisby, making Moira and Arthur laugh.

"Speaking of dinner," said Moreover, "it's your turn to cook tonight, Moira. Remember?"

"Sure. I'm making goosh pie," said Moira.

"Goosh pie!" exclaimed Arthur, laughing.

Moira looked at Arthur.

"I've got a pet snake," she said. "Do you want to see him?"

"No," said Arthur, trying out the truth.

Moira grinned.

"Come to our house for dinner." She looked up at Moreover. "Is that all right?"

"Come, come," said Moreover, starting for the car.

Arthur looked up at his aunt and uncle.

"Go ahead," said Aunt Elda, smiling.

"We're having asparagus soup for dinner," whispered Uncle Wrisby. "Go."

Moira took Arthur's arm and pulled him to the car.

"Pile in back," called Moreover. "But mind the mouse."

"Mouse?"

The backseat was filled with boxes, tools and a doc-

tor's black bag. As Arthur watched, a small field mouse appeared from under the front seat to sit on Arthur's shoe. The mouse sat up on his back legs and pushed his nose up in the air.

"Where did he come from?" Arthur was delighted.

Moira turned around to kneel on the front seat facing him.

"Somebody didn't want him," she said. "So Moreover took him home."

"But he likes the car," said Moreover. "Moreover, as many times as I carry him out, he sneaks back in. Don't know how."

Arthur knew how. He looked down at the floor and saw the road through several large holes.

"Here we go!" shouted Moreover. The car coughed and began moving. Arthur turned to look out the back window. He waved at Aunt Elda and Uncle Wrisby, and watched as Pauline flew from the side yard and began chasing the car.

"How do you say 'go home' in French?" asked Moira, laughing. "Wish I had a French dictionary."

Pauline stopped running then and pecked at the road, the car forgotten.

Arthur looked at the mouse now sitting on the seat beside him.

"*I* wish I had my journal," he said fervently.

And he and the mouse stared at the road as it moved in gray swiftness beneath the car.

Mouse

By the time they reached the Hotwater house, the mouse was sitting in Arthur's hand. Its nose twitched, and its fur was flat and smooth. He could feel the heartbeat when he closed his fingers around it.

"Here we are," said Moreover, and the car skidded sideways in the gravel road. The mouse ran up Arthur's arm and hid in his shirt pocket.

Moreover disappeared, bag in hand, inside a large white house with yellow gingerbread trim. And Arthur was left in the sudden silence of the car, a captive with Moira, the starling. She turned around and looked at the mouse in his pocket.

"What do you do, Mouse?" she asked.

"Arthur," corrected Arthur. "What do you mean do?"

"I mean Mouse," said Moira with a beady stare. "What do you like to do?"

"I write," said Arthur, sighing.

"Write," repeated Moira thoughtfully. She turned around and pulled up her socks. "I wrote a school theme once about my uncle who was an orphan and murdered three goats."

"He what? He really?" Arthur sat up with alarm and the mouse burrowed down further in his pocket.

"I made it up," said Moira. She pushed her hand across her nose, snuffling. "I got an A. Except for spelling, that is."

"You made it up?"

"Sure. Don't you make things up?"

Arthur thought. "Not usually. I write the things I think about—the things that happen to me."

Moira stared at Arthur for a moment. Then she shrugged her shoulders.

"Maybe," she said, "you ought to try making something up for a change. Sometimes it's more interesting."

It was Arthur's turn to stare at Moira.

"But it's not real then," he said.

"Oh, real," scoffed Moira, turning around and bouncing impatiently on the seat. "What's real?"

A sudden memory of the mockingbird poem went through Arthur's head. *Which one's the mockingbird? which one's the world?* He opened his mouth to say something, but before he could speak Moreover opened the door of the car, and a large yellow-haired dog jumped in the backseat. He looked at Arthur, nosed Arthur's hand, then collapsed across the seat, burying his head in Arthur's lap.

"He smells bad," said Moreover behind the wheel.

Arthur smiled slightly. The dog did smell bad. Terrible. He looked up at Arthur, his eyes dark. The mouse moved in Arthur's pocket.

"You've got a way with animals," said Moreover, looking over the front seat. "Moreover, that mouse is yours now. A gift from me to you. Ever thought about being a vet?"

Arthur hadn't, but he had a sudden vision of himself surrounded by sick animals. Some with bandaged legs, some on crutches. No. Arthur stifled a laugh. Not crutches. Broken legs, wings, perhaps.

"He smells like garlic," said Arthur, who rather liked garlic.

Moreover turned his head to one side, sniffing, and the car barely missed a large gray boulder by the road.

"I think you're right," he announced. "Moreover, that means he's been getting into garbage."

Moira turned around again and peered at Arthur.

Does she always, he thought, *ride backward in the car? My parents won't let me ride that way. It's dangerous. But she never bumps her head when the car stops. And she's about to say something. Again.*

"You know what you look like?" asked Moira. She bent her head to one side. "I mean *who* you look like with the dog's head in your lap? Just like your uncle and Bernadette."

Arthur knew that. He had just been thinking the same thing. He moved uneasily beneath the dog, and the dog wagged his tail, thumping it loudly against the door. And Arthur rode to Moira and Moreover's house with a smelly dog in his lap, a mouse in his pocket and a vague, uneasy feeling in his head.

The MacAvin house was mostly porch and was half white and half brown.

Arthur looked at Moira, and she shrugged her shoulders, sensing his question.

"Can't remember," she said, "whether Moreover was painting a white house brown or a brown house white. It was a long time ago."

Arthur was impressed. His family never left anything undone. His father always put his tools away. Always picked up his work clothes. His mother always washed the dishes right after eating. Always. Always.

Inside, the house was full of homemade furniture and braided rugs. Arthur knew the furniture was homemade because of the way the tables and chairs leaned. He'd made a bench once out of old pine that leaned just the way all the furniture did in the Mac-Avin house.

Moira opened the door to her room.

"What happened?" cried Arthur.

"What do you mean what happened?" asked Moira, frowning. "Nothing happened. This is my room."

Sturnus vulgaris, thought Arthur, remembering the Latin words for starling in his bird book. *The starling's nest,* he remembered, *is filled with messes of weeds, twigs, string, feathers, cloth . . .*

Moira's room was littered with books, clothes, tools, paintings, pieces of wood and piles of yarn and food.

"Shovel a place to sit, Mouse," said Moira.

"Arthur," said Arthur. He moved a plate with part of a dried-up cheese sandwich on it and sat on the bed. Moira plunged under the bed and came out with knitting needles and blue yarn. She began casting on stitches.

"I'm making a bedspread," she said to Arthur. "How many stitches do you think I'll need?"

Arthur looked at the cluttered bed.

"Hundreds," he said, smiling. "Hundreds of thousands, maybe."

"Fourteen hundred and thirty-six," said Moira positively, her tongue stuck out of the side of her mouth. She smiled back at Arthur.

"Why that number?" he asked.

"I like it. Don't you have a favorite number?"

"A favorite number?" asked Arthur slowly. "I guess I never thought about it." He watched her cast on stitches for a minute. "That's a lot."

"It doesn't really matter," said Moira, suddenly serious. "I'll never finish it, you know." She put down her knitting and got up to look in the mirror. "Actually," she said, peering intently into the glass, "I'm thinking about making braces for my teeth. I have some silver wire here."

"Making braces!" exclaimed Arthur. "You can't do that!"

"And why not?" asked Moira, turning around. "Just you tell me why not," she repeated a bit fiercely.

"Moira," called Moreover. "Time to start supper."

"Let's go," said Moira. "You'll like my goosh pie." She hurried out the door. "Come on," she yelled from the hallway.

Arthur got up and looked in the mirror. *And why not? Arthur asked himself. Why not?*

"Actually," he began softly, talking to himself in the mirror. "Actually," he called louder as he went out the door to find Moira, "I've always liked the number forty-two."

Moira and Arthur made braces, and Moira practiced talking, teeth clenched and grinning. Arthur kept his in his pocket. They ate Moira's goosh pie, which was really beef stew, in bowls that tilted sideways on the slanted kitchen table. Moira's braces slipped, and they laughed into their mugs of milk.

At home that night, Arthur watched his mouse disappear and appear again from its new home, a hole beside the fireplace. Then Arthur took his braces out of his pocket and slipped them around his teeth. He grinned at himself in the mirror. His hair was uncombed, and with his smiling face, he didn't look much like Arthur anymore.

I look, he thought happily, *a little bit like a mouse.*

Secrets

Aunt Elda saw life up close. Arthur watched her gather flowers, clutching them close like secrets, her face buried in the blooms. He saw her with her hands wrist deep in bread dough, kneading, patting and caressing; her fingers fluttering like small birds, lighting on Pauline, touching Arthur's hair, Uncle Wrisby's arm.

Aunt Elda also had a close and personal battle with the devil, whom she called Ears. He lurked behind every door and woodpile and within every misfortune. She shook her fist at him, whispering, cajoling, threatening.

"You tell him, Arthur," she said while Arthur stood smiling self-consciously. "Arthur knows you're here, Ears, you red rascal." She put her hands on Arthur's shoulders, enlisting him in her war.

Arthur was intrigued. He found himself peering behind doors and walking cautiously through the hallways at night, fancying more than once that he glimpsed the whisk of a long red tail.

Ears' home, thought Arthur, if he did live at Aunt Elda's, was her mammoth iron stove; her fiercest foe, her adversary. Sometimes Aunt Elda was the victor, baking lemon meringue pies with tops untouched by ugly black specks. Sometimes the stove won, sending off billows of smoke that sat on the cloud-white windowsills and dulled the leaves of Aunt Elda's plants.

Of all the chores that Arthur did, opening up the door at one end of the stove and feeding slabs of wood to the fire was the most exciting. He pictured Ears there, crouched and grinning, ready to be refueled. Arthur stared into the fire twice, and once slammed the door with such a sudden rush of fright that Aunt Elda gave the stove a kick with her boots.

"Himself is right behind you, Ears," she admonished. "Beware."

Himself was Aunt Elda's name for God. Arthur's parents never talked about God as a "Him." Arthur's mother talked about trees, earth and sky in a most confusing way. As someone who only prayed in emergencies, Arthur felt absurd saying "Please make Piggy Rathbone stop beating me up" or "Make my parents stop arguing" to a tree. He felt better having an honest-to-goodness devil around with Himself close behind.

Before every meal Aunt Elda had a chat with Himself. Uncle Wrisby read the newspaper, rustling it when she took too long.

"Okay," said Aunt Elda, settling down to business.

"We could use some hot weather, we've had enough rain. But not too humid, please." Nothing was beyond the realm of Himself. "And keep watch over . . ." A list of names followed, including Arthur, Arthur's mother and father, Arthur's cousins and aunts and uncles, Uncle Wrisby, Moira, Moreover, Bernadette, Pauline, and with extra feeling she would add, "And do what you can about Yoyo Pratt."

"Beans have stopped steaming," prompted Uncle Wrisby, peering around his newspaper.

"Church tomorrow," said Aunt Elda, unruffled. "And no making change from the collection plate, you hear?"

"But a whole dollar, Elda!" protested Uncle Wrisby.

"A whole dollar and pass the applesauce," said Aunt Elda firmly.

"Do I go to church, too?" asked Arthur.

"Of course. Everyone goes."

"Even Moira?"

"Even Moira and Moreover."

"Can I take my mouse?"

"Sure," said Aunt Elda. "Himself doesn't care."

"How come Himself cares about my whole dollar?" boomed Uncle Wrisby.

Moreover came the next morning to pick them up for church, but Aunt Elda insisted on driving, and she sat behind the wheel dressed in a flowered dress, a small white hat with one of Pauline's feathers sticking in it, and her low-topped walking boots. Pauline perched up in the back of the car to look out the rear window.

The church was small and white, with a spire painted green. Swallows flew out from the belfry, swinging down over the crowd and wheeling up to disappear in the louvers.

Reverend Railbaugh stood on the steps, greeting his congregation. He had a shiny, bald head and a small, jutting-out chin beard that bobbed up and down as he spoke. Arthur watched it, fascinated. The sermon was long and Reverend Railbaugh spoke very precisely—so precisely that no vowel escaped his close attention, no consonant was left unspoken to its fullest.

"Lettt usss sssing hymn numberrr one twenty-sixxx," spat Reverend Railbaugh.

Arthur thought about the Reverend's garden laid out in paths as precise as his sentences. Moira and Arthur kept count of his beard bobbings on their church bulletins. Arthur had the most.

"You counted salvation as three bobbings," accused Moira in a fierce whisper. And they practiced saying sal-va-tion while feeling their chins.

"Neitherrr cassst ye yourrr pearrrls before sssswine," intoned Reverend Railbaugh.

At the mention of swine, Moira poked Arthur.

"I have a book for you," she whispered. "Later."

After Uncle Wrisby was awakened and Reverend Railbaugh had hissed the benediction, Moira and Arthur ran off together. The sun beat down on the gravel road, and they stopped once to give Arthur's mouse some water from the brook.

"Let's cut in to the pond," said Moira. "We can wade."

She led the way, pushing suddenly off the road. Arthur put a hand over his pocket to protect the mouse as the branches swept back. Moira was a lone walker, not used to having someone follow.

Soon they came to a clearing. A meadow stretched out with a small pond at one side. It was the pond Arthur had seen through the binoculars, but up close it was different. Buttercups had not yet gone by, and there were forget-me-nots on the bank making a blanket of sky color. They lay down, trailing their feet in the cool water. Arthur wished he had brought the binoculars. He wanted to see the house. And he wanted to see if the tree outside his window looked smaller.

Moira pushed her feet down into the mud of the pond bottom, and slid her fingers through the plants of the bank. Arthur had a sudden vision of Aunt Elda. *They're the same. Moira always sits into the earth as if to root there. Aunt Elda becomes part of the bread dough.*

Moira sat up and began putting her socks on wet, muddy feet. Arthur winced.

"Let's go to my house for lunch, Mouse."

"Arthur," said Arthur automatically. He carefully wiped his feet on the grass.

"We can have sliced-strawberry-and-sugar sandwiches," said Moira. "And I'll get you the book I told

you about in church. It's a book on birthing pigs."

"A book?" Arthur looked up at her. "Why do I need a book?"

"Because," said Moira, turning to push through the path, "sometimes pigs need help."

"Help!" exclaimed Arthur. "But Uncle Wrisby knows what to do!" He hurried after Moira, who had disappeared into the woods.

"He even sings to her," called Arthur, nearly running into Moira, who waited patiently at the road.

Moira nodded.

"Sure he sings to her."

"He loves her!" insisted Arthur.

Moira nodded again and began walking down the road, kicking a stone before her.

"I know, Mouse," she said softly. "But just because he loves her doesn't mean that he'll do what she needs." She stopped suddenly and looked at Arthur. "Look at my mom and dad. My dad left in the fall. 'Be back before you know it, Moira,' he told me. He never came back. My mom said she was leaving here forever. For better things." Moira sniffed. "She comes back all the time. But only for money from Moreover."

Arthur stood still, so still that he could hear the soft burbling sound of the brook. He had never thought about Moira with parents. Moreover seemed enough.

"Come on." Moira's voice intruded in Arthur's thoughts. They walked awhile in silence until they came to Moira's house. They walked through the animal room first. There was a cat with three kittens, all asleep; two young opossums with their noses poked curiously up in the air; and a dog with a cast on its front leg. The dog whined, and Moira put a small bowl of water in its pen.

"Not too much," she told the dog, breaking their long silence. "It might make you sick."

They went into the kitchen and Moira began slicing the strawberries. As Arthur watched, he thought about Moira's parents and his own. *Both leaving us. But not the same kind of leaving.*

Mostly he thought about Moira telling him about her parents. Something important, shared. And suddenly, something inside Arthur seemed to move, to shift, to open up a bit like a door opening in a dark room and letting in a sliver of hall light.

"Moira," he began, his voice firm and sure as if bestowing a gift of his own, "my mother is going to have a baby."

Meaningful Questions

There was a long silence, a stillness in the room so that the ticking of the wall clock and the sound of Moira's knife slicing strawberries became unbearable for Arthur. He held his breath, at the same time shocked and relieved that he had finally told someone about the new baby. *Not just someone,* thought Arthur. He had told Moira.

"And?" prompted Moira, looking up from the strawberries.

Arthur let out his breath. "And? And that's it!" he finished lamely.

Wasn't that bad enough? Or was there something more? Something worse about babies than he already knew from books. Something unprintable.

"I don't want a baby," said Arthur, suddenly angry.

"So don't have one"—and she added pointedly, "when you grow up. This one's your parents'." She popped a strawberry in her mouth and screwed up her

face. "Sour," she said. She looked at Arthur thoughtfully. "Ever know a baby?"

"Of course. And I've written down all the things I've
seen about babies."

"I said *known*," said Moira. "Not seen." She put down
her knife. "You know something, Mouse, that's your
problem. You spend so much time writing in that journal of yours that you don't really see what's going on
around you."

"Arthur," said Arthur. "What kind of things?"

"You sound just like the social worker, Mouse," said
Moira, sighing. "Always asking meaningful questions."

"Arthur," repeated Arthur. "What's a meaningful
question?"

"*That's* a meaningful question." Moira's voice rose.
"She asks meaningful questions like 'What do you
think about?'; 'Do you get angry easily?' and 'How do
you feel about yourself?' Then," said Moira loudly,
"she writes it all down in *her* notebook! Just like you!
And you know what, Mouse?" Moira was shouting
now. "She just writes it all down. She never does anything about it. Just like you! Never . . . doing . . .
anything!" Moira's hand upended the sugar bowl, and
it fell to the floor, shattering, the sugar spread out
around the broken pieces. Moira began to cry, her face
buried in her hands.

Arthur was not certain he had ever seen a girl cry
before. At least not right in front of him. But Moira was

not embarrassed. She let it go on awhile as Arthur stood, fidgeting, not knowing what to do.

Finally he spoke. "The social worker," he began softly. "What does she write down? Why does she come?"

Moira looked up at Arthur, her face strawberry streaked. "She comes to check on Moreover and me. Because my parents don't take care of me. To see"— Moira took a breath—"to see if I should go to a foster home."

"A foster home. With a stranger?" Arthur asked, incredulous. "Moreover wouldn't let that happen. He cares about you." His voice sounded high and tight. "Doesn't he?"

"Yes," said Moira in a whisper. "He cares. But he cares just like he cares about that dog in there." She swung her arm toward the animal room. "That's the third time he's been here this year. The third time! Moreover keeps patching him up and sending him home to be hit by another car. Next time he'll die. Don't you see?" she cried. "Moreover once said you can't care too much, don't you know, or it hurts too much later. Later when what you care about is gone."

Moira sat down at the table, her head on her arms.

"Like Uncle Wrisby," Arthur said slowly.

Getting close, he thought. *But only so close. My parents not telling me about the baby.*

He looked quickly at Moira.

"The far away end," he whispered to her. "Maybe

that is why Uncle Wrisby looks through the far away end of the binoculars." He smiled and moved over and put his arm around Moira. He had never put his arm around a girl before. For a moment he thought about it. Then, as Moira snuffled, he pulled his arm tighter and didn't think about it anymore.

"Moira," he said after a while. "I'm hungry."

Moira nodded her head up and down.

"Moira," he said after a moment. "I hate strawberries. They make me shiver when I eat them."

For a second, Arthur thought Moira was crying again. Her shoulders began to shake and she made snorting sounds. But then he realized she was laughing.

They both laughed while they swept up the sugar, picking up animal hairs from it, deciding what sugar could be saved and what thrown away. And they laughed while they ate their sliced-strawberry-and-sugar sandwiches. Arthur shivered through two sandwiches, and they ended up with sugar mustaches.

They cleaned the kitchen, then the front room and dining room because the social worker was coming soon.

As Arthur left, he paused with his hand on the door. "I'll do something," he said to Moira. "You'll see. I *promise* I'll do something."

Moira held out the book on pigs.

Arthur sighed and took it. And as he walked down the front path he heard Moira's gentle laughter behind him. He walked thoughtfully, not noticing the moon that came up behind him. And he nearly stepped on the heels of Uncle Wrisby.

"Arthur, is that you?"

"Yes."

"Been to Moira's?"

"Yes."

Arthur took a deep breath.

"Uncle Wrisby? Moira loves Moreover. A whole lot."

Uncle Wrisby nodded. "Yes she does. And Moreover loves her."

"But he doesn't let her know how much he cares, Uncle Wrisby."

Uncle Wrisby looked down at Arthur.

"Maybe he doesn't say it, Arthur. I figure that for Moreover it's more in the doing."

The doing.

"After all, Arthur, how many people tell those they care about just how much they care?"

Arthur smiled. *Boy, Uncle Wrisby,* thought Arthur. *Now* that's *a meaningful question. And you know something? I love you.*

It came as a great surprise to Arthur, and it wasn't until Uncle Wrisby reached over to take Arthur's hand that he realized he had said "I love you" right out loud.

The frogs started their night noises, a whippoorwill startled them with its song—so loud—nearby, and they walked the rest of the way home with the moon.

Roses and Onions

"Letters for you," called Uncle Wrisby at the back door.

Arthur looked up from the oak table where he was eating lunch and reading. Uncle Wrisby handed him two letters, one in the rangy script of his father, the other on blue paper with the stamp upside down (upside down for "I love you") and the straight-up-and-down half printing, half writing of his mother.

"Thanks." Arthur stuck them in the back of his book and went on reading.

Aunt Elda looked at him curiously from the sink. But she said nothing. He had received five other letters from his parents, also unopened. Arthur had left them on the cupboard top where they sat, silent still as if there were no words written within. Finally, they had mysteriously appeared in his room on the night table, where he had slipped them into the drawer, still unread.

"What's that?" asked Uncle Wrisby, folding himself into a chair. "Another journal?"

Arthur shook his head and turned the book around for Uncle Wrisby to see.

"When Your Sow Has Babies," read Uncle Wrisby. "A book! What's a book gonna tell about sow babies?" he scoffed.

Arthur pushed his sandwich away. This "doing" business wasn't easy. It was not pleasant reading about pigs at lunchtime, either, especially the chapter he was now reading entitled "The Omnivorous Pig," followed by a full-blown description on the subject of "when to let your young pigs slop freely."

"Uncle Wrisby, when are Bernadette's babies going to be born?"

"I'd say," said Uncle Wrisby, peering at the wall calendar over his glasses, "in about three weeks."

"Three weeks!" exclaimed Arthur, sitting up straight. "That's soon! And it says here that she ought to be in a grass area of her own, all fenced off from the other animals."

"Says where?" asked Uncle Wrisby loudly. "Show me where." He pushed his chair around the table to sit next to Arthur, studying the picture of a huge, contented pig in a pen. "Bernadette's been birthing for years, and she never had a fenced-off place like that. All she needs is love and singing."

"But do you know what could happen?" began Arthur. "It says right here . . ." And Arthur began listing the problems in the book. But Uncle Wrisby was no longer listening. He'd picked up his garden galoshes, taken his sandwich and gone quietly out the door.

Aunt Elda sighed and sat down in Uncle Wrisby's chair.

"Don't mind him, Arthur," she said. "He just doesn't like to know about such things, the bad things that could happen. He figures that if he doesn't know about it, it won't make him worry. Or if he doesn't know about it"—she looked at Arthur— "that maybe it won't happen at all."

"But that's silly," protested Arthur.

"Maybe it's silly . . . maybe it is," said Aunt Elda softly. "But I think, Arthur, that you understand." She reached over to his book and pulled out his parents' letters. "Don't you?"

She put the letters on the table and got up to wash the dishes, leaving Arthur to stare at the familiar but not so familiar handwriting on the envelopes.

Uncle Wrisby was in the side garden, hoeing between the rows of onions and roses, when Arthur found him. The hoe turned up the sweet, dark, wet earth and made the garden a strange mixture of smells: a bittersweet smell of new dirt, of the flowering tree blooming at the corner of the garden—Arthur tried to remember to ask what it was—and of onions and roses.

Uncle Wrisby knew Arthur was there. Arthur had seen him look up, briefly, as he approached. But he said nothing, continuing to turn over the earth between the plants in a slow, steady movement.

Arthur watched for a while, then he sat down between two onions, willing to wait until Uncle Wrisby came to that place, either to hoe around him or to bring the hoe down through Arthur's jeans.

Uncle Wrisby came to Arthur and stopped.

"Oh, all right, all right," he said gruffly, and sat down in the pathway, his knees coming up to his chin. He took a drink from his bottle of medicine, then hit his chest with a fist.

"Heart," he said, peering over his glasses at Arthur.

Arthur nodded. Then on impulse he mimicked Uncle Wrisby. "You mean because you got one or it's ailin'?"

Uncle Wrisby looked sharply at Arthur, then threw back his head and laughed.

"Uncle Wrisby, I want . . ."

"I know, I know what you want," said Uncle Wrisby, waving his hand. "You want to build a fenced-off place for Bernadette. Okay, okay, go do it. Fencing is in the barn. Metal stakes in the shed. But it's hard work."

"I'll do it," said Arthur excitedly. "I won't complain."

"Darn right you won't," said Uncle Wrisby, getting up to hoe again. "Bernadette won't like it anyway," he muttered. "All she needs . . ."

"I know," said Arthur, suddenly grinning at Uncle Wrisby. "All she needs is love and singing."

Arthur jumped over a row of roses, then a row of

onions, then stopped. "Uncle Wrisby?"

"Yep." Still hoeing.

"How come you planted a garden of onions and roses?"

Uncle Wrisby straightened up and rubbed his back. "I like them."

"Roses are nice," agreed Arthur.

"But they got thorns," warned Uncle Wrisby. "Take onions, though." Uncle Wrisby pushed his glasses up on his forehead and gazed lovingly at his onions. "You can plant them, touch them, smell them *and* eat them." He smiled at Arthur. "Not like books."

As Uncle Wrisby began to hoe again, Arthur let his eyes unfocus on the garden. He could still see the roses, looking like watercolor flowers in the background. But now he saw the tall, dark-green onions, standing like sentries in a row.

Arthur smiled to himself. It was almost like looking through the far away end of the binoculars. Far away, but near somehow. He shook his head a bit to clear his eyes.

Look one way, look the other, he said to himself, remembering the poem Aunt Elda had read to him.

As he walked to the barn, the mockingbird flew from inside, trailing hay from his beak. He stopped to watch the bird circle over and fly above the barn, then fly back again to the tree outside Arthur's bedroom window.

I wish, he thought, *I wish I could unfocus my eyes just enough to make that tree look smaller. Then maybe I could climb it.*

Arthur stood for a moment, trying to make his eyes work the way he wanted them to, but no matter how hard he tried the tree looked just as tall as ever.

Finally, he shook his head, closing his eyes for a brief time. Then, opening them again, he went inside the barn to find the fencing for Bernadette.

Sounds

Even though Aunt Elda began to ask Himself for rain—
"Not too much please, no cloudburst needed"—none
came. And the summer days and nights grew uncom-
fortably warm and still. Arthur read his pig book long
into the night, making notes in his journal, his mouse
watching the movement of his pencil across the paper.

Monday, June 28: The birthing sow should have a
private bed of dry hay with a warm light nearby.
When the pigs are delivered they will automatically
turn to the light for comfort. This way all the babies
may be delivered safely, then put to the sow for nurs-
ing. Even the best of dams has been known to crush
one or two young by mistake.

The sow should have a private pen for the last
week before birthing. This way, she may feed on
clean pasture and be out of the way of other animals
when she begins to give birth.

Pauline woke Arthur each morning, clucking at his pillow and pulling at his hair, and she watched him outside as he began to build a pen for Bernadette.

Putting up a fence was hard work, much harder than Arthur had ever imagined. Moira came to help him carry the heavy roll of fencing outside, Pauline running in wild excited circles around them. The wire was sharp and made deep, painful grooves in Arthur's hands. Aunt Elda found bandages and gloves, then left Arthur and Moira to build the run. Uncle Wrisby, true to what he had said, left them alone. No help—none asked for. Their bargain. A hard bargain, Arthur was beginning to think.

"Now," asked Moira, sitting on the roll of wire, "how big should the pen be?"

"Oh, from about here"—Arthur paced off a length—"to about here."

Moira smiled. "You have to measure, Mouse. You have to plan."

"Arthur," said Arthur, frowning. He had never planned anything in his life. For Arthur, everything happened one way or another, either the way it should or the way it shouldn't with no help on his part. He watched as Moira walked off a plot of grass, taking giant steps. She took a piece of paper from her pocket and borrowed his pencil, and when she was through there was a drawing of a long run, metal stakes three feet apart.

Together, they pounded in the first two stakes while

the sun rose higher. Pauline ran under the shade of the tree and sat watching them. Arthur looked up once to see Uncle Wrisby, leaning on his hoe, watching too.

"Is it lunchtime yet?" whispered Arthur, wiping his forehead.

Moira straightened up and made shades out of her hands, looking at the sun.

"I'd say," she said, sounding very much like Uncle Wrisby, "it looks about ten o'clock."

Arthur sighed.

"Not lunchtime," he said. And they pounded in two more stakes, rested, then measured, then pounded in two more. Then it was lunchtime.

Bernadette lay in the far corner of the paddock as they passed by. Arthur climbed up on the wooden fence to look at her, Moira beside him. Pauline flew up and settled between them.

"Bernadette," Arthur called. "You are going to have a new grassy pen all your own."

Bernadette didn't move. She twitched her tail to scare away a fly, but she didn't even open her eyes.

"You ungrateful old sow," murmured Arthur, making Moira laugh.

"Do you want a thank-you, Mouse?" she teased. She peered closer at him. "Is that what you're looking for?"

"Arthur," said Arthur, suddenly cross. "I told you I'd do something. I'm doing it." He climbed down from the fence and walked to the house, wondering just what it was that he did want. But most of all, throughout the quiet lunch with Moira, Arthur wondered why he was building the pen for Bernadette.

Moreover was in the paddock when Arthur and Moira came outside again. He felt Bernadette's sides, putting his ear next to her bristly skin, listening. He looked up to see Arthur and Moira standing next to him. He pointed to the pig book under Arthur's arm and smiled. "So that's where that book got to."

"Moira gave it to me."

Moreover nodded and took out his stethoscope. "This is for show," he whispered to Arthur. "My ear has already told me that there is a wild group of snorts in there just waiting to be born."

Arthur laughed and knelt beside Moreover.

"They're a wild group, all right," Moreover repeated. "Moreover, after they're born they'll have to have iron shots and proper pasture so they don't get the thumps."

"The thumps!" exclaimed Arthur. "What are the thumps?"

"Improper feed," said Moreover, "can cause the thumps. It's a pig sickness. Moreover, it can be serious." He got down on all fours and demonstrated, jerking his hindquarters while Arthur and Moira shrieked with laughter. Arthur took out a small notebook that he had learned to carry and wrote:

The thumps: Baby pigs can get the thumps. Can regular babies get them too?

Arthur put away his notebook and touched Moreover's sleeve. He nodded at the stethoscope.

"Can I listen?"

Moreover handed him the stethoscope, and he placed it on Bernadette's side. At that moment, all the sounds of the day seemed to stop for Arthur: the rustlings and pawings of the other animals, the sound of Uncle Wrisby's hoe in the garden and the ever-changing song of the mockingbird. A new sound made him still with excitement. Arthur moved his head a bit to see Uncle Wrisby in the garden, still working. Strangely, like a movie with no sound, he saw the action but heard only the soft and mysterious turnings of Bernadette's babies inside her.

He was startled when Moira tapped his shoulder to listen, too, and he stood up, grinning, while Moreover grinned back at him. There were many questions he wanted to ask, but Arthur couldn't speak. He looked down to see Moira smiling at the same sound he had heard. Finally he looked at Bernadette. Somehow she didn't look so ugly to him anymore. Arthur looked at her wet snout, her bristly ears.

Why, he thought, *she looks . . . she looks . . . almost pleasant.*

Five Dollars Even

On Wednesdays the Yoyo Pratt of Aunt Elda's prayers came through the valley selling things from his donkey cart. The cart was painted red, had an old umbrella top and was pulled by a very nasty donkey whom Yoyo affectionately called Jack the Ass. Jack would kick anyone who came close enough, and when approached from the front, he would pull his lips back to show his teeth.

Yoyo was the very picture of a villain. He had a black mustache that curled up at the ends and had one slightly yellow eye. It was said that he chewed adult aspirins. Yoyo wore a long gray coat, even in the warmest weather; the envy of every child in the county, for it had many pockets—twelve to be exact. They were full of nails, small wooden toys, sewing thread, nail clippers, perfume, jewelry and dried soup. All for sale. The cart held secondhand clothes, canning jars, fresh fruit and vegetables (and *nearly* fresh fruit and vegetables), writing paper, metal pots, books, wooden spoons, yarn, cold remedies and anything anyone wanted to be rid of or buy.

"Sooner or later, everything's bound to come back to me," Yoyo was fond of saying. "Just like the yo-yo comes back to the hand." On his cart was a sign that said:

Use It for a Little While
Then Yoyo Buys It With a Smile.

Aunt Elda didn't like Yoyo one bit.

"He's greedy, mean to his wife, and he smells like cream of celery," she grumped. "And he could sell sewing needles to a porcupine."

"Elda knows," bellowed Uncle Wrisby.

"Oh, hush," said Aunt Elda.

She grabbed a broom and swept at Arthur's and Uncle Wrisby's feet, pushing them out the door.

Outside Jack turned to sneer at Arthur, and Pauline ran from the side yard, head stretched out, to peck at Yoyo's boots.

"Blasted chicken!" yelled Yoyo, kicking at her and running behind the cart. Jack shifted and rolled his eyes. Yoyo's coat flew out behind him as he ran, and Pauline grabbed it with her beak.

Uncle Wrisby and Arthur laughed.

"You'd better learn some French, Yoyo," called Uncle Wrisby. "*Allons! Arrêtes,* Pauline!"

Pauline stopped, and Yoyo slunk out from behind his cart, eyeing her.

"I'll make French casserole out of that rascal some-day," he threatened.

Uncle Wrisby's eyes narrowed to slits. "Don't you ever talk that way about Pauline. Ever," he said softly.

Arthur looked up, surprised. He'd never heard his uncle talk that way. So softly, yet so firm.

"Now, now, Wrisby. Just a joke," soothed Yoyo nervously. "Come, come. I have a new batch of your medicine, fresh from the pot. Two dollars and twenty-five cents a bottle."

Aunt Elda came out to buy pickle jars, a dollar a dozen, and Arthur looked through the cart. There were no prices written on anything, and he soon discovered that if he asked Yoyo the price more than once, it could go up or down depending on Yoyo's mood. It was like a game, knowing when to stop and when to ask again.

"This top, Mr. Pratt?"

"Seventy-five cents, Arthur. And call me Yoyo."

"How much is the animal book, Mr. Yoyo?"

"One dollar and fifty-nine."

"And the top?"

"Fifty cents even, boy."

So it went, a game of sorts amid a tangle of treasures.

"Ah," said Aunt Elda in a soft voice. So soft that they all looked up.

She picked up a piece of glass and held it up to the light.

"A prism! Like Aunt Mag's. I'd almost forgotten."

Aunt Elda moved the prism, and it caught the sun and tossed sprinkles of colored light across Jack's wide back and Yoyo's cart.

Arthur saw the look on her face. "Aunt Mag?" he asked. "Who is Aunt Mag?"

Aunt Elda looked at Arthur for a moment, a measuring look. Then she shook her head, one slight shake of dismissal. "Sometime," she said. "Sometime." She gazed at the prism, then without looking up she asked, "How much, Yoyo?"

"Six dollars," said Yoyo.

Aunt Elda sighed and put the prism back in the cart. There was a silence as they watched her walk up the path and into the house.

"Well," said Yoyo finally. "Anything you want?"

There was something Arthur wanted. The minute he had seen the long canvas case he had known what was inside. His mother had a recorder, a wooden one, that she kept in such a case. Once she'd let him play it, showing him how to finger some of the notes. He remembered the mellow, sad notes that had made the hair on his neck rise when his mother had played. He also remembered the rasping squawks when he had played.

Arthur pointed to the case.

"What's that?"

Yoyo opened the case and took out the recorder. He held it upside down, blower end down. Arthur felt the

first pricklings of excitement in his stomach. Yoyo didn't know what it was.

"Looks like a musical instrument," said Yoyo slowly. "Five dollars even," he announced briskly.

Arthur forced himself to look at a box of fish hooks. He forced himself to think about the money in his pocket. Three dollars and seventeen cents. "How much are the fish hooks?" he heard himself ask. His throat felt dry.

"Thirty-five cents."

Arthur hesitated. "How much is the canvas case? Without that thing . . . the instrument?" asked Arthur.

"The case alone?" asked Yoyo, surprised.

"It would be just right for my knives and pencils," said Arthur.

Uncle Wrisby smiled and folded his arms, leaning on the cart. He looked at Yoyo.

"Well," said Yoyo, turning the case over in his hands. "I guess this case looks like a dollar."

"Okay," said Arthur. He felt in his pocket and counted out a dollar. "Do you want an old rag or something to wrap the wood thing in?"

"Sure enough," called Uncle Wrisby. "Those things are kind of delicate. You might not be able to sell it if the air got at it too much."

"Oh, drat," complained Yoyo. "More trouble than it's worth."

Arthur started toward the house to find a cloth. Then he stopped.

"If you want," he called, "I'll take it off your hands for, say, fifty cents."

"Seventy-five," said Yoyo promptly.

"Oh, all right," said Arthur. His hands shook as he counted out the money.

Yoyo grunted his thanks and climbed back up on the cart.

"I'm late, Jack the Ass," he called. "Git up!" The donkey backed up, snorted and flattened his ears. Then the cart rattled off down the road. Yoyo turned once to look at Arthur and Uncle Wrisby. Then he was lost around the bend.

Uncle Wrisby began to laugh. He laughed all the way up the path to the front steps. He took off his glasses and wiped his eyes. He hooted and slapped his pant leg. Arthur began to laugh, too.

"Yoyo," said Uncle Wrisby, stopping to catch his breath, "will get all the way to the Hotwaters' house before he realizes that he sold you a 'five dollar even' recorder for one dollar and seventy-five cents." He took the bottle of medicine out of his pocket, drank some and hit his chest with a fist, still laughing. "You know, Arthur, I should have bought the bottle and had Yoyo throw in the medicine!"

Aunt Elda came out of the house to see what the noise was about. Then she shooed them off to feed Bernadette.

"You should have had Arthur buy the pickle jars for

you, Elda," he called over his shoulder. "Yoyo might
have thrown in the lids!"

This put Aunt Elda in a wicked mood, and there was
cold beet soup for supper with a hot dish of cut-up
greens that Arthur suspected were dandelions. But he
didn't care. He had his recorder.

After supper he hurried to Moira's house to show it
to her. Pauline came after him, clucking softly behind
him.

"Pauline, *vite!*" urged Arthur impatiently. He looked
back once. *"Vite!"* he called crossly, and Pauline came
after him, running in slow and fast spurts.

"Why, Mouse," exclaimed Moira when he showed
her the recorder. "You are really doing things."

"Arthur," said Arthur. He frowned. "You don't
think Yoyo Pratt will think I cheated him, do
you?"

"Not Yoyo," said Moira positively. "That's the way
he does his business. That's the way he is."

Arthur practiced the recorder all evening, sitting
cross-legged on his bed. But there was a soft prickling
of worry, like the beginnings of a sore throat, something other than his mother's baby or Bernadette's babies. And it wasn't until early dawn that Arthur sat
upright in bed, suddenly awake and knowing what it
was. Pauline had not come home with him.

He ran downstairs and looked behind the stove.
Pauline wasn't in her cradle. Her blanket wasn't even

warm. Arthur searched the yard and the barn, but Pauline was nowhere.

Finally he went to Aunt Elda and Uncle Wrisby's bedroom, feeling sick with dread. He knocked at the door, and when Aunt Elda opened it, Arthur burst into tears.

"My fault," he sobbed. "She's gone. I've looked everywhere."

Aunt Elda gathered Arthur up in her arms while he blurted out the story. He laid his wet face against Aunt Elda's big, white night braid. And Uncle Wrisby threw on his clothes and went out in the stark morning light to look for Pauline.

The Casserole Threat

Arthur cried and Aunt Elda sat with him in the great wicker rocking chair by the bed. They could hear Uncle Wrisby calling Pauline outside, his voice sometimes far away and muffled, sometimes as close as breath on the window glass.

"It was my dumb recorder," said Arthur tearfully. He sat up suddenly. "All I could think about was that recorder and playing it. *And* showing Moira I could do something." He stood up and ran upstairs.

"Arthur," called Aunt Elda. She pulled her cotton robe around her and went into the hall.

Arthur appeared with his recorder. He ran into the kitchen, opening the devil's end of the stove.

"Arthur!" shouted Aunt Elda at the top of her voice.

Arthur stopped, his hand on the stove door. Aunt Elda never shouted.

"You'd better chop it into smaller pieces," she said softly.

"What?"

"Here. Here's the hatchet. Go chop the recorder into pieces so it will burn better. That will be more likely to bring Pauline back home."

Arthur closed the stove door. He felt foolish. "I have to do something," he said helplessly.

"I've got a good idea," said Aunt Elda. "If it makes you feel better, go upstairs and throw the recorder out the window. Then put on your clothes, go get Moira and find Pauline."

Arthur went over to Aunt Elda and threw his arms around her middle.

"I'll find her. I promise," he said, his voice muffled in the softness of her robe.

Upstairs, his mouse sat on the stone hearth, looking at him solemnly as he opened the big window and threw his recorder out. He looked down to see it lying in the flower bed. He felt better.

Uncle Wrisby was in the kitchen when Arthur came downstairs. Uncle Wrisby looked pale and thin, his long fingers clasped around a cup of tea. Aunt Elda made Arthur eat some toast.

"Arthur," she said before he went out the door. "Pauline's been gone before."

Arthur knew that she was trying to make him feel better. But when he looked back through the window, he saw Uncle Wrisby put his arms around her.

They're afraid, he thought. *They're afraid just like me.*

The valley rang with French, and they rustled the bushes, calling.

"Bonjour, Pauline. *Où es-tu?"*

"Pauline! *Viens!"*

Moira knew no French, so Arthur gave her the French phrase book, and she called "Where is the restroom?"; "How old is your favorite uncle?"; and "Do you wish fresh towels brought to your room?" all in French.

"Maybe it doesn't matter what you say," said Arthur sadly. "As long as it's French."

They circled back to the gravel road again and walked toward Uncle Wrisby's.

"Maybe I'll go over to the Reverend's," said Moira. "Sometimes Pauline goes there for millet. You could try Yoyo Pratt's. Maybe she followed his cart."

It was then that Arthur suddenly remembered and told Moira about Yoyo's threat: the casserole threat.

"He'd never really eat Pauline!" said Moira, indignant.

"But how do you know?" asked Arthur, miserably. "You're the one who told me that you could never tell what people would do. When you told me about your parents." His voice softened. "Do you remember?"

Moira said nothing. But Arthur knew she remembered. They both sat still, the noises of the day surrounding them, closing them in. Finally, Moira got up. She went over to touch Arthur's arm.

"I think," she began softly, "we'd both better get over to Yoyo's."

Arthur got up, his heart pounding. The sun was high overhead, and Arthur saw that it would be clear. The brightness of the day bothered him. He wished it were raining or gray. Chipmunks ran along the stone walls, plunging down, then popping up between the stones to watch them on their way to Yoyo's house. They stopped once to look at a large spiderweb stretched across the side of a juniper. It was shaded from the sun, still shining with the wet of early dew. But they just looked at it, not speaking.

Yoyo's house was a small, gray saltbox with weathered shingles, almost dwarfed by the large lilac bushes that grew around it. A larger barn stood behind, with Jack's cart waiting in front.

"See the cart," whispered Moira. "That means he's leaving."

The bush hid them well. Arthur sat with closed eyes and smelled the strong, sad scent of lilacs. He opened his eyes when he felt Moira stand up to look in the window.

"It's the kitchen," she whispered, pushing his head down. "There's a pot boiling. I can see the steam."

A pot. Arthur stretched up beside Moira just as Yoyo came in the kitchen door. They ducked down quickly, together, and crouched.

"Pot's simmering, Maggie," they heard Yoyo call. "Hurry up."

The palms of Arthur's hands felt wet. He rubbed them along his pants. "What's in the pot, Moira?" he asked.

"Can't see," she whispered. "They're leaving, though. Wait."

Moira moved closer to Arthur and looked over at him. She reached out her hand and Arthur took it. He looked down at the big fist they made.

They heard the sounds of Yoyo yelling at Jack, then the grating of the wood plank across the barn door. The cart rattled, and from their hiding place, they watched it move slowly down the road. Yoyo drove, with Maggie sitting straight beside him.

Moira took a breath.

"Okay," she said, her voice sounding suddenly loud. "I'm going in to look at the pot."

Arthur stood up. "I'm going, too."

The kitchen door wasn't locked, and they walked into the room. Dismayed, Arthur saw that the table was set for supper: two blue-flowered plates and silverware.

Moira lifted the lid and peered into the pot. She took a large fork, stretched up on her toes and poked the contents. Then she carefully closed the lid again.

"It's a chicken, Mouse," she said.

"Oh, no," said Arthur. He felt tears at his eyes. "What can I say to Aunt Elda and Uncle Wrisby?" he cried.

Moira didn't speak.

Arthur looked down at the table, staring at the plates. Then, angrily, he picked them up, along with the silverware, and put everything back in the cabinets.

"Yoyo's not going to eat Pauline, that's for sure," he said in a trembling voice.

Moira nodded.

"Let's bring the pot, too," said Arthur, his voice breaking. "We'll have a proper funeral."

Moira searched through the drawers and found two pot holders. She handed one to Arthur. And they walked out the door and down the road, each holding a handle of the pot.

Arthur began to cry, quietly. He was glad that Moira didn't say, 'Don't feel bad,' or 'Everything will be all right.' He knew he would feel bad forever. But worse—much worse than feeling bad forever—he'd have to tell Aunt Elda and Uncle Wrisby about Pauline. Silently, they passed by the spiderweb in the juniper, now almost invisible in the sunlight. When Uncle Wrisby's barn came into view, Arthur felt a sharp jarring in his stomach.

"Wait," he cried out.

They put down the pot by the side of the road.

"I can't," moaned Arthur. "I can't tell them. I can't."

Moira touched his shoulder. "You can," she said softly. "You have to." She bent down and put her hand around one of the pot handles. "Lift."

Together they picked up the pot and walked slowly past the barn and turned into the yard.

"Arthur!" called Uncle Wrisby from the barn. "Where have you been?"

Aunt Elda opened the kitchen door and hurried out.

"We've been calling and calling you," she said. She stopped when she saw the tear smudges under Arthur's eyes and the look on Moira's face.

Arthur went over to Aunt Elda and put his arms around her.

"She's gone." He lifted his face to look up at Aunt Elda's face. "I'm sorry. So sorry." He began to cry against Aunt Elda, his chest hurting and his body shaking.

"Arthur," said Uncle Wrisby softly. He came over and untangled Arthur from around Aunt Elda. "What are you talking about?" He brushed Arthur's hair from his eyes. "She's not gone anymore." He turned Arthur around and pointed his long finger toward the paddock fence. "See?"

A flash of rust flew to Arthur's feet and began pecking his shoelaces. Brisk, hard pecks that hurt.

"Pauline!" cried Arthur.

"It is Pauline!" shouted Moira.

Aunt Elda put an arm around Arthur.

"We looked and called for you all morning," she said. "We found Pauline sleeping in the tree outside your window." She pushed Arthur's hair back and wiped at his cheeks with her apron.

Arthur began to laugh and cry at the same time as Pauline pecked happily at his shoelaces. He knelt down and picked her up, burying his face in her feathers. He couldn't remember, ever, being so happy.

"Oh, Pauline," he said softly. *"Je t'aime."*

Later, Arthur brought Pauline a pan of water and watched her drink. She tilted her head back so the water could run down her long neck.

"Never," he promised her, "never again will I forget you."

Suddenly Uncle Wrisby raised his head and sniffed. "I smell goose."

Moira looked up from where she sat beneath the tree. "Goose?" she said. "I don't smell goose."

"Well, I know goose smell when I smell it!" insisted Uncle Wrisby firmly.

There was a silence. Moira and Arthur stared at each other.

"Oh, no," said Arthur, breathlessly.

"It's Yoyo's chicken," cried Moira. "I forgot all about it!"

"That's no chicken!" boomed Uncle Wrisby. He followed his nose around the tree until he stood over Yoyo's tipped-over kettle, Bernadette's nose pushing the lid into the grass.

"Goose," announced Uncle Wrisby positively. "Greasy goose, too." Uncle Wrisby slowly folded his arms and looked down at Arthur and Moira. "No made-up stories," he said sternly.

"We thought it was Pauline," blurted Moira.

"Pauline!"

Arthur nodded. "Yoyo said he'd eat Pauline if she didn't stop chasing him. Remember?" he implored.

"We went to his house," said Moira. "There was a pot boiling." She pointed. "That pot. Mouse here wanted a proper funeral."

"Arthur," whispered Arthur automatically.

Uncle Wrisby, arms still folded, walked off a bit and stared up the road while Moira and Arthur waited uneasily. Then Uncle Wrisby swung around. He stooped beside them, his long arms gathering them in.

"Now," he whispered. "Here is what we'll do."

Thursday, July 8: It has been a long day. Uncle Wrisby went to bed early. To sleep off his day of crime, he says. Aunt Elda kept saying PRAISE BE when we told her what we'd done and what we had to do. She was mad because she'd been cooking a chicken all day long, and what we did meant hot dogs for supper (only Aunt Elda calls them franks). Uncle Wrisby must be the most brilliant person alive, and we told him so. It made him happy, but it made Aunt Elda say PRAISE BE three times in a row. We couldn't put the goose back because Bernadette had nosed it into the dirt. So we took Aunt Elda's chicken, put it into Yoyo's pot and carried it back to Yoyo's house. It was as simple as that. Maybe not that simple. We put the pot on Yoyo's stove and turned on the burner. Then we left. Then I remembered that I had to go back and set the table again. Then we left. Then, all

of a sudden, Uncle Wrisby felt his nose and said, OMIGOD I LEFT MY EYEGLASSES AT YOYO'S. This time it wasn't so easy. Just as we got there Yoyo's cart came up the road. We hid behind a stone wall wishing we knew what to do when Uncle Wrisby stood right up and pulled us after him. He ran up to Yoyo and said, I WAS JUST WALKING BY YOUR HOUSE WHEN I SAW BIG AS LIFE A FURRY THING PUSH OPEN YOUR SCREEN DOOR AND WALK INTO YOUR HOUSE. LOOKED LIKE A WEASEL. Mrs. Yoyo screeched lots of real long screeches, and Yoyo galloped old Jack up to the barn. I'LL GO IN FIRST, yelled Uncle Wrisby, and he ran into the kitchen while Yoyo ran to the barn for his rifle. Mrs. Yoyo stood up in the cart and kept yelling and lifting up her skirt and jumping from one foot to the other as if she expected the weasel to run out, reach up and steal her patent leather shoes right off her feet. Pretty soon Uncle Wrisby came out and shrugged his shoulders. CAN'T SEE THE CRITTER, he called to Mrs. Yoyo, BUT SUPPER SURE SMELLS GOOD! He grinned at us, pulled out his glasses and put them on his nose, and we walked home. We had a supper of hot dogs (franks), and then we had a funeral for Yoyo's goose. We buried it in the back field and put flowers from Aunt Elda's front garden on its grave. No one could think of much to say except for Uncle Wrisby. He said, THANK GOD YOU WEREN'T PAULINE. Aunt Elda said, PRAISE BE.

The Prism

Summer days grew too hot for play, so Arthur and Moira worked on Bernadette's pen in the mornings. In the afternoons they stayed close to Uncle Wrisby's cool barn, Arthur lying in the hay, stroking Pauline, watching her closely for signs of distrust.

"Does she know?" he asked Aunt Elda one day. "Does she know it was my fault?"

"Maybe, maybe not," replied Aunt Elda promptly. "But it's no matter." She turned to look at him. "She's forgiving."

Was it his imagination or did Aunt Elda mean that he was not? He thought of his parents' letters upstairs in the drawer under his journal.

"I'm sorry," he murmured to Pauline. "I'm sorry," he said again, startling himself, wondering why he'd said it so loud.

Pauline tilted her head from one side to the other looking back at him.

Does she see differently out of each eye? How do I look to her?
He took out his small notebook and read the note he
had written there:

Look one way, look the other.

He thought a moment, then took his pencil and
wrote one sentence.

How do my parents see me?

Arthur stared at the sentence a long time, so long that
his eyes began to water and the letters blurred. Then he
closed the notebook and held it tightly as if he had to
keep the words from escaping.
"*Viens,* Pauline," he called. And he picked up Pauline
and went out into the sunlight to work on his pen.

On Sunday morning, early, when the daylight was
still behind the trees, Arthur and Moira finished the
pen. They sat back under the big tree and grinned at
each other, sweat and dirt streaking their faces. The
pen was large and shiny, with a gate and heavy gate
latch that Uncle Wrisby had silently helped them at-
tach.
Aunt Elda and Uncle Wrisby came out of the kitchen
door with juice and hot biscuits for them. Uncle Wrisby
was half dressed for church, black pants and black sus-
penders over a clean white shirt. And bare feet. He

went to get Bernadette while Aunt Elda admired the pen.

Uncle Wrisby opened the pen door and tapped Bernadette gently. Bernadette stared at the lush green grass and the shady place at the end. Then she backed away and turned to root in the main paddock.

"Come on," Uncle Wrisby called to Moira and Arthur. "You'll have to help get her inside. She's shy about new things."

Arthur and Moira leaned on Bernadette's backside and muttered to each other through clenched teeth.

"Push!" grunted Moira fiercely.

"I *am* pushing," hissed Arthur.

But Bernadette would not move.

Uncle Wrisby knelt in the far corner and crooned "Come All Ye Fair and Tender Maidens," beckoning. But Bernadette eyed him suspiciously and stood still. Finally, he sang her very favorite song, *"Plaisir d'Amour,"* his voice sounding strong in the soft morning light.

> *"Plaisir d'amour ne dure qu'un moment,*
> *Chagrin d'amour dure toute la vie. . . ."*

Pauline clucked on the fence, but Bernadette stood, solidly, resisting their tugs, pushes and songs.

Aunt Elda brought her most odoriferous slop, and Arthur dug up a shady part of the pen, pouring buckets of water to make cool, oozing mud. But Bernadette was not interested in slop or mud. She was not interested in the new pen. She regarded Arthur through placid eyes, and backed slowly into the main paddock.

Arthur was inconsolable.

"I *finally* did something," he said mournfully, "and it didn't make any difference at all. She hates the pen."

Uncle Wrisby put his arm around Arthur.

"Give her time, Arthur. Give her time to get used to the pen."

"She hasn't *got* time!" lamented Arthur.

Uncle Wrisby turned Arthur around to face him. "It's a fine pen, Arthur," he said firmly. "A very fine pen."

"A fine pen," Arthur insisted, shaking off Uncle Wrisby's arm, "is not an empty pen." And he walked off, leaving Moira, Aunt Elda and Uncle Wrisby looking after him.

They stood silently until Aunt Elda, with a small sigh and a lifting of her shoulders, walked quickly and caught Arthur at the back door.

"Arthur," she said softly.

Arthur stood by the stone step, but didn't look up.

"Maybe you ought to think about why you built the pen."

"Why?!" Arthur turned around. "I know why."

"Because," persisted Aunt Elda, "if you built it for Bernadette you have to be content with what Bernadette decides. And give her time to decide. Maybe, Arthur, you didn't really build it for Bernadette after all."

Arthur stared at Aunt Elda.

"You know," said Aunt Elda, putting her arm around Arthur and walking inside with him, "Aunt Mag used to say that the reasons we do things are sometimes not what we think they are. And"—She held up her hand as Arthur tried to protest—"everything we do makes a difference. Some kind of difference."

Aunt Elda opened the polished mahogany doors of the downstairs parlor and took Arthur to the fireplace. She pointed to an old picture in a gilt frame on the mantel.

"Aunt Mag," she said. "You would have loved her. We all did. The children first. The grown-ups didn't know how much they loved her until later."

"But—" Arthur began.

"Don't interrupt," said Aunt Elda firmly. She gave the picture to Arthur and sat down in an overstuffed chair.

"When Father Caleb's wife, Violet, died giving birth to her youngest, he was left with two older children and a small, weak newborn baby."

"What did she die of, Aunt Elda?" asked Arthur, aware that he was interrupting.

"Of childbirth, Arthur. Many woman died in those days having their babies. Caleb grieved for many days. Violet had been a delicate and soft-haired woman—a child herself—too weak for having another child. Caleb ran off for several weeks, living in the woods, suffering and drinking while the family cared for his children. The aunts and uncles had their own families, of course, and their own farms to keep, so they were hard put to do all the caring for Caleb. So one of his brothers found Caleb in the woods and brought him back to his problems."

"How old were Caleb's other children?" asked Arthur.

"Oh, Tris was twelve, I guess, and Mandy ten. Your age, Arthur. They had their schooling and their friends, so they had some things to comfort them. But the burden of caring for the baby fell to them. After school and chores—and they had many chores—they would have to feed the baby. And to love it. The loving part must have been hard, because that same baby was the very thing that had killed their mother. But they raised it and loved it. When the baby was about four years old, Caleb saw that he couldn't burden them with the housework, the child and all the chores any longer. So he wrote a newspaper ad for help."

"For a housekeeper?" asked Arthur.

Aunt Elda shook her head. "No," she said. "For a wife."

"A wife!" exclaimed Arthur. He looked at the picture and saw a strong-faced woman with steady eyes.

"That's when Aunt Mag came," said Elda. "She traveled from far away, a sailing town on the coast of Maine. There were many mail-order wives in those days, Arthur."

"And the children liked her?" urged Arthur, smiling.

"From the very moment she walked up the front

steps of the house, raw-boned and tall. She was taller than Caleb, even. She looked at Tris, I remember. He was the oldest, and so frightened. 'You're going to be very tall,' she said gruffly. 'Like me.' That pleased him. Then she reached into her black satchel and took out a rose-colored ribbon. Satin it was. She wound it around Mandy's long hair. 'Rose is your color,' she said. 'We will sew you a rose dress.' "

Aunt Elda smiled, remembering.

"And then she took the youngest one on her lap. From her handkerchief she took a piece of glass. A prism. She held it up to the light, and it sent colors everywhere in that drab room. 'You won't remember your mother,' she said, 'but you will learn that her life touches yours. All of us touch each other. Just like the colors of the prism. Don't you forget that.' "

Aunt Elda took the picture of Aunt Mag. "And I never did," she said.

Arthur looked quickly at Aunt Elda. "You! You were the baby?!"

Aunt Elda nodded. "Then she washed our ears and made us scrub our knuckles until they were red. We loved it! And she read to us every night and showed us how to make dyes from wild flowers and taught us about music. She told us stories about the sea and where she came from; and about birds and how some of them migrated—hundreds of miles sometimes—and how some of them never left home.

"Like the mockingbird?" Arthur asked softly.

"Yes, Arthur, like the mockingbird. Her hair was coarse and thick, and a wonderful cloud-gray color. She used to leave it out for the birds. She left yarn pieces outside, too. How we loved to find a nest with the yarn wound about. The older family scoffed at her at first, Arthur. Her ways were different, you know, and her way of speaking." Aunt Elda leaned forward, her eyes bright. "But you know one day I found Caleb behind the shed with his knife, cutting pieces of his hair for the birds! And Aunt Mag showed Caleb how to make dandelion wine in an old crock." She put her hands on her cheeks. "Oh, the smell of that wine, with cut-up lemons and oranges in it! All the aunts and uncles came over to taste it one afternoon. It tasted so good that they drank it all day and into the evening." She leaned over close to Arthur. "They all had to stay over for two nights, they got so tipsy and ill! And Aunt Mag took care of everyone, never scolding. From then on, even Caleb grew softer with her. And when he got sick, Aunt Mag plowed the fields. She'd hook up the horses and harness and plow. Never complaining."

"I wish I had known her," said Arthur softly.

Aunt Elda looked at Arthur. "Well, if what Aunt Mag said was true, then you do know her, Arthur. She touched me." Aunt Elda reached out her hand and put it on Arthur's arm. "I touch you."

Aunt Elda got up and put the picture of Aunt Mag back on the mantel.

"Aunt Elda," said Arthur slowly. "Do you think that

Aunt Mag would think . . . That is"—Arthur took a
deep breath—"do you think that I built that pen for
myself?"

Aunt Elda smiled at Arthur. "She might have
thought just that, Arthur. What do you think?"

Arthur looked at the picture of Aunt Mag. "I think,"
he said, "that maybe Uncle Wrisby was right. Moira
and I built a fine pen."

Aunt Elda's smile widened. "Well now," she said.
She walked over to an old bureau and dug down into
a drawer. "Here's something—a gift—to always remind
you of what Aunt Mag said. And what you know."

She handed the cloth-covered object to Arthur.

"From Aunt Mag to you," she said.

She walked to the door and turned. "Tell the old man
to get ready for church," she said, and she walked out
of the room and up the stairs.

Arthur unwrapped the cloth carefully so as not to
break what he knew was inside. He held the prism up
as he walked to the window, watching as sudden colors
spiked across the ceiling and around the room.

He thought about Aunt Mag and Aunt Elda cutting
their hair for the mockingbird.

I always look the same, Aunt Elda had told him.

Arthur thought about the bird carefully weaving the
hair in his nest.

We were both wrong, he thought. *Aunt Elda doesn't look the
same at all anymore.* Nothing *looks the same at all anymore.*

And when Arthur slept that night, his head was filled

with many thoughts—of babies, a mockingbird, a nest with long yellow-white hair and short gray hair, a motherless child, a tall woman from Maine and dandelion wine. His thoughts fused together and crisscrossed, lighting up his dreams.

Like a prism.

Doing

"I'm going shopping in town!" called Aunt Elda. "Want to come?"

Arthur looked up from the breakfast table as Uncle Wrisby walked into the kitchen carrying Pauline.

"Don't you think Pauline looks pale and peaked?" he asked.

"How can a chicken be pale and peaked?" scoffed Aunt Elda. But she looked Pauline in the eye. *"Qu'y a-t-il?"* she asked.

"Maybe Moreover had better take a look at her," said Uncle Wrisby. *"Viens*, Pauline. *Va dormir."* Pauline jumped from his arms and ran to her cradle, pulling the bit of flannel over her.

It made them all smile, the familiar comfort of it.

"I'll stay with her while you go to town," said Arthur eagerly. "I'd like to take care of her. Please?" he begged. "Moira will stay too. And we'll keep an eye on the pigs."

"Well," said Uncle Wrisby. "That does make sense."

"Everything about Wrisby's pigs makes sense," said Aunt Elda, putting on her hat. She smiled at Arthur. "All right, Arthur, but we'll be away for lunch."

"We'll fix our own lunch," said Arthur. "And I'll take good care of Pauline this time. I promise."

"Of course you will," said Uncle Wrisby. "Here come Moreover and Moira now."

Later, Arthur and Moira watched Moreover's car waver off down the road, small puffs of smoke leaving a trail behind it.

"Now," said Arthur decisively, turning to Moira. "Do you think Pauline looks pale and peaked?"

Moira shrugged. "She's not pale. What does peaked mean?"

"I don't know," admitted Arthur. "Maybe she's tired. How much sleep does a chicken need?"

"Moreover says a sick animal may need a tonic," said Moira. "Can I eat a cucumber?"

"Sure. What's a tonic?"

"I think it means medicine," said Moira. She peeled a whole cucumber in the sink and sat down to eat it.

"Wait," said Arthur, suddenly remembering the medicine sitting by the sink. Uncle Wrisby's medicine. He picked it up, pointing to the label.

"Tonic," he said happily. "It says tonic."

"Then give her some," said Moira, licking her fingers.

"I don't know" said Arthur, hesitating. "I'd better taste it first."

"Oh, for heaven's sake," said Moira. "Can I have another cucumber?"

"Well, I don't want to give her anything that won't be good for her," reasoned Arthur. He tilted the bottle and sipped some tonic. He made a face.

"It's terrible!"

"Let me try," said Moira. She drank some. "It's not bad. Tastes like fruit."

"Let me try again," said Arthur. "You're right," he said after drinking. "It does taste better now."

He poured some in a small saucer and gave it to Pauline. She dipped her head down and back several times.

"She likes it!" cried Arthur.

Pauline did like it. She flapped her wings and drank again.

"You know, it is good," said Moira. She drank some more, thoughtfully chewing her cucumber between drinks.

The two of them drank for a few minutes, then they filled Pauline's dish again. Pauline flapped her wings, flying to the table and back to the kitchen counter again.

"She's better!" said Arthur, delighted. He felt wonderful, too. Quite brave and wonderful.

They drank some more, Moira dipping her cucum-

ber into the tonic until she suddenly noticed the time.

"I've got to go home," said Moira, jumping up. "Moreover said early today."

"I'll come too," said Arthur. He picked up the medicine bottle, and Pauline flapped after them.

"See?!" he exclaimed. "She really likes it."

On the way to Moreover's house they laughed and sang *"Plaisir d'Amour"* in loud voices. Once they stopped under a tree to catch their breath and drink more medicine. Pauline fluttered up next to them and they shared it.

They came to Moreover's house, stumbling across a hydrangea bush and falling, giggling, up the front steps. The door opened for them, and Moreover stood there, looking very tall and stern.

"I'm here," said Moira loudly. "See!? Sorry if I'm late." And she tripped over the top stair with Arthur tripping behind her. He fell on top, with Pauline flying in over their heads.

Moira laughed. "Get up, Mouse. I can't move."

"Arthur!" said Arthur, laughing back at her.

"Moira!" Moreover's voice was strained.

Moira heard the tone, and she pushed Arthur off of her. Then, they both saw the woman with the brief-case. Arthur heard Moira cry, "The social worker!" And then she stood up and threw up all over Moreover's black Sunday shoes. When Arthur saw that, he threw up, too.

"Why they're sick," exclaimed the woman with the briefcase. "The chicken's sick, too!"

Then Moreover smelled them, and he knew what they didn't know.

"Whisky," he announced. "They are sick, ma'am; moreover, they're drunk."

And then he took Moira over his knee and spanked her so hard that Arthur began to cry. Moira cried, too. But it was different.

"Oh, Moreover," she cried joyously between sobs, "you *do* love me!" And she threw her arms around him and held on.

The woman came over to Arthur and put a wonderfully cool cloth on his head as he lay there. He pushed himself up on one elbow.

"I'm sorry," he said feebly. "I wanted to make Pauline feel better. So I gave her Yoyo's tonic."

"Hush," said the woman softly.

"And we thought we should taste it first." He started to cry. "I've been *doing*. Moira said I should be *doing* things."

"And you have," said the social worker in a soothing voice. "You have."

Arthur slept fitfully. When he awoke, he was in his own bed, and his thoughts were a tangle of pictures and talking: Moreover with his arms, tightly, lovingly, around Moira; Uncle Wrisby telling him "a fine pen"; and strangely, his mother reaching out of the car to put her arms around him saying, "I love you, too."

The strong light from the windows made him wince, and he turned over to burrow beneath the bed covers. The sudden movement made his head hurt.

"Arthur?"

He peeked out of a fold of quilt to see Aunt Elda sitting by his bed, Pauline on her lap.

"Are you feeling all right?" she asked. She set Pauline on the bed and the chicken settled on a pillow, giving Arthur's outstretched hand a soft peck.

"I'm all right," said Arthur miserably, closing his eyes again. It was hard to talk, but he forced himself to ask the question that was there between them.

"Moira and Moreover?"

"Fine," said Aunt Elda. Arthur could tell she was smiling, but he made himself look at her to make sure. She was. "She sent you a note. Do you want to read it?"

Arthur sat up gingerly and took the note.

Dear Mouse,

Are you O.K? Becaus Moreover and I are O.K. We are getting to know each other better. The socail worker said we are fine. Fine together, that is. This one promised not to ask meeningful questions. She knows Moreover loves me. *I* know Moreover loves me. That's pretty meeningful, isn't it?

Do you know what I feel like, Mouse? A baby.
That's what. A baby starting out from the beginning.
Thanks, Mouse.

Love,
M.

Tears stung Arthur's eyes. "Boy," he said after a
minute. "Moira sure is a rotten speller." And he lay
back on the pillows and fell asleep again.

The next time he opened his eyes, Uncle Wrisby sat
in the window seat, looking out the window through
his binoculars.

"The funniest thing," said Uncle Wrisby as if he had
been talking to Arthur all the while. "I believe this
mockingbird is building a nest in the hedgerow by the
barn."

"I'm sorry, Uncle Wrisby," said Arthur.

"Goes without saying," said Uncle Wrisby briskly.
"Goes without saying."

When Aunt Elda came upstairs later with juice for
Arthur, he asked her what Uncle Wrisby meant.

Aunt Elda smiled. "It means 'I know what you're
saying' or 'I know what you mean' or . . ."

"Or I love you, too," said Arthur.

"That, too," said Aunt Elda matter-of-factly.

After she went downstairs, Arthur lay for a long
time, thinking. His mouse peeked its head out of a

small chink in the fireplace. He got up and gave it a piece of cheese, and it disappeared into the chink again. Arthur lay down with his face to the hole, trying to see in. He thought about the moles beneath his parents' lawn. He thought about eating peanut-butter-and-lettuce sandwiches with his father and the way his mother walked when she was in a hurry. He got up and dressed. Then he found a pen and paper.

Dear Mom and Dad,
    My summer has been fun. I got drunk and threw up. It's my fault that Pauline got lost, too.
                            Love,
                            Arthur

No, that wasn't right. Too long. He tore up the letter and began again.

Dear Mom and Dad,
    Everything is fine here. I'm not drunk anymore.
                            Love,
                            Arthur

He tore that letter up, too. He didn't want them to worry. Or did he? He frowned. He finally wrote:

Dear Mom and Dad,
    Things will get better. It goes without saying.
                            Love,
                            Arthur

"Mouse!" There was a knock at the window, and Moira pressed her face against the glass.

"Moira!" Arthur ran happily to the window and opened it. "You came the tree way."

"I brought some watermelon gum," said Moira, sitting comfortably in the tree. "And some of my cookies to make you feel better."

They both laughed, for Moira's cookies were always horrible, either too crumbly or too hard or without sugar. These were hard. Arthur found a hammer and pounded them into sucking pieces.

"I'll come in," said Moira, poking her head in the window.

"No. Wait!" said Arthur suddenly.

Moira stopped and sat back on the tree limb.

"I'll come out there."

With only a moment's hesitation, Arthur crouched on the windowsill. Then, carefully, he crawled out onto the limb and over to where Moira sat.

He smiled at Moira.

"Now," he said with his mouth full of cookie and his voice sounding only the slightest bit frightened, "tell me how it is to start all over again like a baby."

Small Changes

The wind began in the night. Arthur awoke to hear the tree branches scraping against the window and the sound of sudden sheets of rain being pushed against the house. By morning the paddock was soggy, and rushing water was making deep ruts at the shoulders of the road.

Uncle Wrisby and Arthur waited for a lull in the storm, then put on boots and slickers and ran through the mud to herd the pigs inside the barn. Bernadette was slow in coming, and Uncle Wrisby urged and prodded her gently. Arthur and his uncle stood for a while in the barn, smiling at each other as the rain and wind began again. Outside the trees bent low and the wind sent waves through the honeysuckle vines covering the stone walls. The wind took Arthur's rain hat and blew it into the paddock. Uncle Wrisby and Arthur ran after it, laughing, as they struggled through the mud.

They dried off in Aunt Elda's fragrant kitchen, holding their hands out above her stove.

"It's going to last a while," pronounced Uncle Wrisby over his teacup. He peered at Arthur. "It may get worse. We're going to town early and fast today. Want to come?"

Arthur shook his head. "I have something to do," he said. "I'll stay."

He looked up, embarrassed, as Uncle Wrisby and Aunt Elda looked at him curiously.

He sighed. "I'm going to read my parents' letters," he said finally.

"Hmn," said Uncle Wrisby, getting up to put on his raincoat, "I reckon that will take most of the day. How many you got there?"

"Wrisby," warned Aunt Elda, smiling at Arthur.

"Twelve," said Arthur.

Moreover and Moira slammed into the kitchen, the wind blowing rain in behind them. Moira's hair stuck to her face. Aunt Elda took a towel and rubbed her dry.

"We'd better get to town," said Moreover. "The road's getting rutty. Moreover, it's getting worse. Moreover . . . "

"Moreover, we're ready," finished Uncle Wrisby loudly.

"Can I stay, too?" asked Moira. "I'll just sit."

"And eat cucumbers," said Uncle Wrisby.

"Come *on*," said Moreover, urging them out the door. "The river's high; moreover, the old bridge planks are rotting out; moreover . . ." His voice trailed away with the wind.

Arthur settled into an old velveteen chair and opened his letters one by one while Moira peeled cucumbers and read old copies of *Hoarde's Dairyman.*

Moira was quiet all the time Arthur read his letters, and when, at last, he looked up, he was surprised that an entire hour had gone by. He read her two, one from his mother telling him about a squirrel who after two weeks had finally become brave enough to eat out of her hand. "Everything takes time, Arthy," she had written. He smiled. His mother was the only one who called him Arthy. Another one from his father told about how his mother had lost her temper after trying to paint a sunset. "She ripped the paper in lots of pieces and jumped up and down on them," he wrote.

This made Moira laugh. "They sound nice" was all she said.

Arthur nodded. "They *are* nice," he said to her and to himself.

Arthur and Moira went to the window, peering out at the storm. For a while, they drew on the windows, breathing on them to make them clean again.

"Mouse," said Moira, suddenly rubbing a pane of glass clear. "Did you and Rasby leave the barn door open?"

"Arthur," said Arthur. He bent his head beside hers

and looked out to the barn. "No. Come on. The wind probably blew it open."

They put on rain gear and pushed the back door open, closing it firmly on a curious Pauline. They ran through the paddock that was now a lake of mud and water. Arthur could feel the mud pulling at his boots as he ran.

Inside the barn, the pigs were in their stalls, restless with the sounds of wind and pouring rain against the barn.

"Where's Bernadette?" asked Moira. "She's not with the others."

"No," called Arthur. "Uncle Wrisby's put her in a stall of her own. Over here." They both leaned over the stall railing and stared at the empty stall.

"The door's open," said Arthur. "Silly pig, where is she?"

"Bernadette!" called Moira.

"Come, Bernadette!" Arthur called louder.

They searched the barn, but Bernadette wasn't there. Not in any of her special places. A loud clap of thunder nearby made them jump. The pigs began to squeal. Arthur looked at the open barn door.

"She must be outside." He took a deep breath. "Let's go." He pulled at Moira's hand.

"I really don't like thunder and lightning," Moira said, standing still.

"And *I* really don't like strawberry sandwiches," said Arthur softly. "Let's go."

Moira smiled, a smile that came and went quickly, and followed Arthur outside.

The rain was worse now, coming in sheets, and they held hands and ran bent over to keep it from hitting their faces.

"Bernadette!" called Arthur.

They stumbled around in the mud, searching the paddock, then stood very still as another flash of lightning and roar of thunder sounded.

"Look!" Moira grabbed Arthur and turned him around. "She's there. See? In the new pen!"

As they began running, another flash of lightning sparked through the sky, and Arthur could see Bernadette standing in the far part of the pen.

"Come!" called Arthur. He neared Bernadette and then stopped, seeing what kept her there.

A tiny pig, flesh-colored with a single dark spot, lay under Bernadette. Its body lay in the mud, and as Arthur knelt to see it more closely Bernadette lashed out with a back leg and turned to look at him. The baby pig lay so still that Arthur thought it must be dead. He put his hand on Bernadette's side to help steady himself, and he could feel her sides heaving and moving.

"Moira?" He looked up. "Go get a rope. We have to get Bernadette out of here. Out of the rain."

"Is it dead?" Moira didn't move.

"I don't know." Arthur looked steadily at her. "Go get a rope!" He shouted the last, and Moira's eyes suddenly came into focus. She stared at Arthur for a moment, then turned and ran to the barn.

"Hanging by the door!" Arthur shouted after her. Then he turned and put out his hand to touch the baby pig.

"Easy, easy," he crooned to Bernadette.

The baby was warm, strangely warm in the cool rain, but it didn't move. He tried to feel for a pulse, but couldn't find one. And then he remembered in the book Moira had given him that he must massage it and keep it warm. Quickly he took off his slicker and then his sweater. He wrapped his sweater around the baby pig. It was so small that it seemed lost in the wool, but he began to stroke its chest.

"There's no rope," said Moira, standing suddenly beside him. She had lost her hat, and the rain plastered her hair into her eyes and down her cheeks.

"Where's your slicker?" she asked, and they both laughed, because they were so wet and it made no difference.

"There's another pig coming," said Moira suddenly, and Arthur saw Bernadette lean toward him.

"Go get a canvas," said Arthur. "Just inside the barn door, covering some hay. Hurry!"

He kept stroking the small pig, and as he watched Moira run to the barn he saw that her shoes were gone. Then he looked down and saw that his boots were gone, too. *I wish I had a warm light,* he thought. *Baby pigs need a warm light.*

Moira appeared with the canvas just as another flash

of lightning made them all seem white and frightened looking.

"The canvas has small ropes at each end," he shouted to Moira. "Try to tie them to the sides of the fence, over Bernadette. We have to keep the rain off." His voice sounded to him like a sob, and he couldn't be sure that he wasn't crying.

Moira began tying the ropes to the fence, first one, then the other, so that there was a small shelter.

"There's nothing to tie the other ends to," shouted Moira, frustrated.

"I know," said Arthur patiently. His voice sounded like his father's, from far away. "You have to hold the other ends over us, like a tent."

He looked down and saw that there were two more baby pigs, alive and wiggling in the mud, then another. He thought, for a moment, that there was another, but then he saw that it was his own bare foot, half buried in the mud. He made an effort and wiggled his toes. "Yes!" he shouted. "It *is* my foot!"

"What?!" shouted Moira, holding the canvas and peering underneath.

"It's my foot!" he repeated.

Moira looked down to where he bent his head, nodded at him, understanding what he meant. She smiled just as two more baby pigs were born.

Arthur continued to stroke the chest of the smallest pig, thinking once he felt the barest of movements, but not trusting himself to stop. The rain came harder, and all he saw was Bernadette and a mass of wiggling, wet babies, and of course, the one he held so carefully in his smelly, wet, wool sweater.

Bernadette began to get up, suddenly, and Arthur shouted at her. "Bernadette! Stop!"

Moira looked under the tent.

"Do something," he yelled at her. "She'll step on them!"

"I can't!" cried Moira. "I'm holding the tent!"

"Then sing!" shouted Arthur, suddenly smiling as he felt the smallest pig, from the depths of his sweater, begin to move. "Sing!"

> *"Come all ye fair and tender maidens,*
> *Take warnin' how you court young men.*
>
> *"They're like a star on a summer's morning.*
> *First they'll appear and then they're gone."*

Bernadette lay back, sinking slowly into the mud, and the baby pigs began to strain to nurse as Arthur and Moira sang. The smallest pig began to kick its feet, and unable to speak, Arthur held up his sweater to show Moira, who grinned and continued to sing, very loud and, Arthur thought, quite a bit off key.

There was a flurry of feet beside him then, and Arthur looked up, seeing Uncle Wrisby's boots and the storm-white face of Moreover peering under the tent.

"It's breathing!" he shouted to Moreover as he lifted

his sweater, still stroking the chest of the baby pig. "It's alive!"

"Arthur did it!" called Moira. "Arthur really *did* it all!"

"Praise be," Arthur heard Aunt Elda's voice as she stooped down to look under the tent. He smiled at her, and wiggled a foot in greeting.

Moreover knelt beside Arthur, his hands gently checking the baby pig. Finally he grinned and nodded at Arthur, holding out his hands.

Arthur handed over his sweater to Moreover, and picked up another lively baby as Uncle Wrisby gently led Bernadette to the barn. He ran to the warmth of the barn and put it down in the fresh, dry hay, then ran back for another. Uncle Wrisby passed him, carrying another, then Moira, then Aunt Elda, barefooted, smiling at him, until all seven babies and Bernadette were in the barn.

Then, while Moreover put the smallest pig—the runt—under a warm light, and Arthur held a bottle of warm milk for it to drink, he looked up to grin at Moira, who had called him Arthur for the very first time.